THE TYC

CW00665439

The only way Caroline could rescue
her brother from serious trouble was to
marry the immensely rich Matthew
Bishop—a fate she was not at all averse
to! But she was far from sure that
Matt, however much he loved her, was
prepared to marry her. Could she
settle for less?

THE TYCOON'S LADY

BY

KAY CLIFFORD

MILLS & BOON LIMITED
15–16 BROOK'S MEWS
LONDON W1A 1DR

First published 1980
Australian copyright 1980
Philippine copyright 1983
This edition 1983

© Kay Clifford 1980

ISBN 0 263 74280 6

Set in Linotype Baskerville 10 on 12 pt.
01–0483

Made and printed in Great Britain by
Richard Clay (The Chaucer Press) Ltd,
Bungay, Suffolk

CHAPTER ONE

CAROLINE HAVELING stared moodily out of the window of her Hampstead flat. Her whole week had been a mess and an exhausting one at that. After a three-day modelling assignment in Paris, she had decided not to take the coach in to Orly but to do some last-minute shopping instead. It had been difficult to find a taxi in the pouring rain, and arriving at the airport damp and weary after being stuck in a traffic jam, she found she had missed her flight. Put on standby, she finally arrived home to find that Jane, her flatmate, had gone to visit her parents, leaving the flat unheated and without food. Shivering with exhaustion, Caroline had found enough milk to make herself a hot coffee drink and had fallen into bed immediately.

The long lie-in she had anticipated was rudely shattered by her brother Tom, who telephoned at seven-thirty next morning.

'What's wrong?' she asked at once, knowing he rarely rose before ten if he could help it.

'I've found a job.'

'Three cheers,' she said dryly.

'Don't cheer yet. My getting it depends on you. I'll need your help.'

'In what way?'

'I'll come over and tell you. See you in half an hour.'

Before she could stop him he put down the telephone, and muttering under her breath she hurriedly dressed and dashed out to the corner grocery shop to get something for breakfast.

She was on her second cup of coffee when Tom arrived. A long, lanky figure, with the same fair hair and blue eyes as his sister, he bounded up the stairs, hugged her and flung himself on the couch.

'Carrie darling, you look marvellous as usual. Obviously hard work agrees with you.'

'It might well agree with you too,' she answered tartly. 'You should try it some time.'

'That's what I want to talk to you about.' He stood up and restlessly paced the room.

Caroline sighed, hoping she had not been disturbed just to listen to another one of his hare-brained schemes for making an overnight fortune.

It was her brother's bad luck not to have been born with a silver spoon in his mouth, though he had done his best to live as if he had, ignoring the fact that, unlike his friends, he did not have family money to support him and would have to make his own way in the world. He was intelligent but lazy, not putting his brain to good use and always full of schemes for making easy money. Occasionally he hit the jackpot, and he then spent his time gambling at one of the numerous clubs of which he was an honorary member—that way he did not have to pay subscriptions!

'Well?' she questioned. 'What do you have to tell me? I can see you're worked up about it.'

'I am. It could be the easiest money I'll ever get the chance of making. You remember Mark Ingle?'

Caroline stiffened. 'Only too well,' she murmured, but Tom carried on, not hearing the interruption.

'We were at school together, but I didn't see much

of him afterwards. His family have mills up north and Mark went straight into the business.' Tom broke off, looking uncomfortable. 'Damn it, I completely forgot! You went out with him for a while, didn't you?'

'Mark didn't mean anything to me,' she lied, 'and it was ages ago.'

There was a pause before Tom continued. 'Well, you know yourself what a decent chap he is. And of course he's absolutely loaded.'

'You don't mean *he's* offered you a job?'

'He's *found* me one. I met him at a party last week. He was with his fiancée—a stunning-looking bird called Helen Warner—and she turned out to be Matthew Bishop's ward.' There was another pause. 'You've heard of Matthew Bishop, I suppose?'

'The name rings a bell, but I can't place it.'

'You must have seen it in the gossip columns. He's Bishop's Industries.' When she still looked blank, he added: 'The millionaire chap who's always linked with the latest swinging beauty.'

Caroline nodded. 'Get to the point, Tom.'

'Bishop *is* the point. He bought out Mark's family firm but kept Mark on the board as part of the deal. They have a large mail order business catering for the cheap end of the rag trade, but Bishop now wants to expand into the better end and sell expensive English and Continental clothes.'

'I read something about it in the papers.'

'It's had quite a bit of publicity, and when Mark was talking to me about it, I had this brainwave. Why shouldn't we cash in on our titles by having an advertising campaign featuring Lord Haveling and Lady Caroline Haveling modelling all these haute couture clothes in various exotic settings? It would certainly create the expensive image Bishop is after.'

'I hate using my title,' Caroline protested.

'I've never understood why. It's the only thing we inherited from the family. For once let's make something out of it. Mark liked the idea and so did Helen, but they couldn't give the O.K. until they'd consulted the great white chief. Then last night Mark rang me and said Bishop liked it too, and could we start on it as soon as possible.'

Caroline frowned. 'Even if I wanted to do it with you, I'm not sure I can. I have commitments for weeks ahead, and unless Penny can revise my schedule or put someone in to take my place, I won't be free.'

'Then the quicker you ask her, the better.' Tom looked at the telephone, but Caroline shook her head.

'I don't like asking favours over the phone. Penny can hold me to those bookings, you know.'

Caroline looked thoughtful, wondering how best to tackle the situation. Penny Grantley ran Grants, one of the top model agencies in the country, and jealously guarded her reputation for reliability.

'Tell her I'll love her for ever if she helps me out,' said Tom. 'Without you, there's no deal for me.'

'I realise that.' Caroline frowned again. Penny had a soft spot for Tom, and it might just be soft enough for her to be obliging. 'How about telling her she can put you on her books? She's always wanted to get hold of a real aristocrat.'

Tom looked alarmed. 'I don't plan to take up modelling as a profession. It's only a one-off thing, more like doing a friend a favour and getting paid for it. After all the idea is mine, and I'm sure Bishop will show his appreciation generously.'

'The arrangements *you* make with him are your own affair,' Caroline retorted, 'but I'm under exclusive contract to Grants and Penny will insist on negotiating my fee herself. You'd be very sensible if you let her handle your fee too.'

'Maybe I will,' he said slowly. 'It would be a sweetener for her.'

'She'll appreciate that. Don't forget it's through Penny that I'm able to help you live in the manner to which you've become accustomed!'

Tom looked apologetic without looking disturbed. 'I don't forget the help you give me, Carrie, and I'm grateful for it. If I weren't such a lazy devil, I'd take a regular job. But the thought of a nine-to-five existence bores me out of my mind.' He grinned at her, then bent and kissed the top of her head. 'Ring me and let me know Penny's reaction. As soon as I hear from you I'll call Mark and fix a date for you to meet Matthew Bishop. I hope it all works out. I don't often get the chance of a free holiday abroad.'

'It wouldn't be a holiday,' she warned. 'Modelling is hard work.'

'We wouldn't be at it all day, though.'

'That's what you think,' Caroline replied, remembering her own trips abroad when she worked from early morning until the light was too dim for the photographers to shoot more film—the idea being to spend as little time as possible on location, to keep expenses to the minimum. If only her brother knew how hard it was to try to look cool in the Spanish summer sunshine as one modelled a mink coat outside the Prado, or posed in a bikini by a sunny pool smiling happily through chattering teeth as if it were a perfect hot summer's day and not a bleak February one. But why disillusion him? Once he started on this project —if it materialised—he would find out for himself.

When Tom had gone, roaring down the road in his secondhand M.G., she poured herself a fresh coffee and curled up on the sofa. If she were honest with herself she would admit that she hated the idea of doing this job with Tom, not because it wouldn't be fun to work with him, but because it would bring her in contact again with Mark Ingle. The thought of him and their last meeting, when he had taken her down to Yorkshire to meet his parents, was still painful.

She had just started to do well as a model when she had met Mark at a party. She had remembered him as a school friend of her brother's and did not mind when he monopolised her for the whole evening.

Although his family business was up north, he had a flat in London, and used it for half the week, during which time he saw Caroline constantly. She had been swept off her feet by his attention, and had found it impossible not to be flattered—even though she was not short of boy-friends—for he was good-looking in a fair schoolboyish way, and knew all the people she knew.

Mark was the first man with whom she had had a sustained relationship, and she swiftly fell in love with him. When he asked her to Yorkshire to meet his parents, she was sure he felt the same way.

Her first and only visit to the large, ugly house outside Harrogate had told her they had no future together. Judicious questioning by his parents had soon established that Caroline did not work for fun, but because she needed to earn a living. They had been impressed by her title, but were the type to be more impressed by money—as was Mark—for after their return to London his phone calls abruptly stopped.

She had been bitterly hurt by his behaviour, and it took her a long while to get over him. The thought of seeing him again was disturbing, but she knew she would have to put herself to the test for Tom's sake. If only her brother were not so irresponsible! Still, perhaps this assignment might give him the impetus to find himself a permanent job.

It was shortly before noon when Caroline parked her Mini on a meter directly outside the agency's office in Davies Street. Luck was with her, she thought, and hoped it was a good omen.

As usual the outer office was crowded with girls waiting for an interview with Penny Grantley, but Susan, Penny's secretary, beckoned her forward.

'How did Paris go?'

'Fine. Is the boss in yet?'

'Do you need to ask? First in, last out,' Susan grinned. 'Go on in.'

Caroline did so and Penny rose to greet her. A model herself—before starting Grant's five years ago—she still had the willowy figure and looks that had brought her to the top of her profession. At the height of her success she had married a wealthy stockbroker who had set her up in business. They had since been divorced and the agency—begun as a hobby—was now her life. She was only thirty-three but already had the hard gloss of the committed career girl.

Caroline explained about Tom's project and to her surprise Penny immediately agreed to see if she could find someone to take over Caroline's bookings during the period she would be occupied with the mail order catalogue.

'Matthew Bishop could put a lot of work your way,' the older girl confided, 'which would mean a fat commission for me! I used to know him quite well. He was a client of my ex and we used to entertain him. Browse through some magazines while I get to work on this. I need an hour or so to set it all up.'

In half that time she had done what she set out to do. Caroline could continue her bookings until she was ready to work with Tom.

'You're an angel,' Caroline said gratefully. 'I don't know how to thank you.'

'I've already thought of a way,' Penny grinned. 'Take over for Madge Moorcroft at Wednesday's show at the Berkeley.'

'I loathe charity affairs,' Caroline protested. 'They're always so hectic and everyone's so bad-tempered.'

'Madge is ill and I have to find a replacement. You were the committee's first choice anyway, so they'll be delighted to have you.'

Knowing she couldn't very well refuse, Caroline nodded and returned home to catch up on the much needed sleep of which Tom's early morning arrival had deprived her.

That night Jane Greigson, her flatmate, told her she was returning to live with her parents. Her mother was not in good health and her father, a doctor, needed Jane in the surgery. Caroline was surprised her friend should want to return to the fold, but soon learned there was more to it than daughterly obligation.

'I rather fancy Dad's new junior partner,' Jane confessed candidly, 'and I've a feeling *he* fancies me. So keep your eyes on the engagement columns of *The Times*!'

'Don't rush into anything,' Caroline warned.

'I'm twenty-five,' Jane replied, 'and unlike you I can't afford to wait for my ideal. Let's face it, once I lose my youthful bloom, what have I got?'

Caroline could not deny the sense of Jane's reasoning. Her friend was pear-shaped and toothy. Yet she was also intelligent and had a great sense of humour. They had been friends since schooldays and when Caroline first started work, Jane had invited her to share the flat and pay any rent she could afford. Now Caroline could manage the upkeep on her own and was pleased at the prospect of having the chance to do so.

The next couple of days passed quickly, with Caroline helping Jane sort out her things for the removal men to crate up, and almost before she was aware of it, it was the day of the Berkeley show.

She was at the hotel by nine, for part of it was being filmed, and it had to be rehearsed thoroughly. Leaving her car in the hotel's underground car park, she went to the ballroom where she was greeted by several other models and the usual pandemonium that preceded any well organised fashion event.

A catwalk had been set up in the centre of the brilliantly lit room, and there was a stage behind it, occupied now by Rick Henderson, a T.V. personality who was acting as compère. Caroline had met him several times and always tried to avoid him, for he gathered information about people like a sponge drawing in water, and was equally adept at spreading it around again. Because of this he was a useful source of information, but a dangerous friend.

After exchanging a few pleasantries, Caroline casually asked him if he knew Matthew Bishop.

Rick looked at her sharply. 'Not taken with him, are you, sweetie?'

'I've never met him.'

'Then steer clear. His ward has first claim on him and she won't willingly let go.'

'My interest is purely professional,' Caroline told him. 'I've been approached by one of his companies and I know he's taking a personal interest in the project. I wondered what he was like.'

'Highly eligible, with three or four million at least, but a bit too rough and ready for you, I'd say.' Rick's eyes were as sharp as his tongue. 'All the girls go for him, of course, and he's never been known to turn down a good offer!'

'I don't expect to make him any offers,' Caroline retorted.

'I've heard that one before. But money is a magnet, my angel, and there's no bigger draw than a fat bank account.'

'Which I'm sure his ward is guarding,' Caroline said lightly.

'With both hands,' Ricky agreed. 'How about a date in exchange for some more information?'

'I don't want any more information.'

Rick looked put out; then his love of gossip won the day. 'Helen's lived with Matt since she was twelve. Her parents were killed in a plane crash on the way to Aintree. Matt was the pilot but came out without a scratch—which did nothing for his guilt complex.'

'I can see why,' commented Caroline.

'He was also a good friend of the wife. A *very* good friend,' he added, 'so that made him feel doubly responsible for Helen. According to rumour, she's now ready to take over where her mother left off, if you get my meaning?'

'But she's engaged to Mark Ingle.'

'Only to try to make Matt jealous.'

'Is he?' Caroline asked, not particularly caring.

'No.' Rick grinned. 'Which only makes Helen all the more bitchy.'

'How do you know all this? Or shouldn't I ask?'

'I never divulge my sources of information, or people would never confide in me!' He gave a wide smile and departed, and Caroline walked backstage slowly, mulling over what she had learned. Although Matthew Bishop was a womaniser, he had had sufficient conscience to make himself responsible for an orphaned twelve-year-old. It would be interesting to see if conscience made him fall for his ward's manoeuvring.

Rehearsals for the dress show went on all morning and it was nearing two o'clock before Caroline and the other models were able to snatch a coffee break and a short rest before getting into their first change of clothes.

Guests had already started to arrive, and the noise of their chatter could be heard backstage, together with the smell of expensive cigars and perfume. There was always a fair sprinkling of men in attendance: husbands or boy-friends of the rich women who made the rounds of the fashion shows and charity affairs in an effort to stave off the emptiness of their lives.

Still, if she had not had to work she might have been one of the so-called idle rich; doing her share of good works between enjoying herself. Yet somehow Caroline doubted it. She had always enjoyed exercising her mind and knew she needed the challenge of a job to give purpose to her life.

The sound of the latest hit record started, and she hurried to change into her first outfit, a white silk suit worn over a scarlet blouse. Each girl had a rail behind her with the clothes she was to model, and after each change the designer and hairdresser came over to ensure that their creation had not been disturbed.

As Caroline waited at the side of the stage for the opening bars that would herald her entrance, she cast another quick glance at the audience. Because of the bright lights she could only see those close to the stage, but her attention was caught by a young girl in the second row, who was carrying on an animated conversation with the man beside her. Caroline could not see his face as his head was turned towards his companion, who was exceptionally pretty, with dark hair, cut boyishly short and swept back off her face in feathery layers. Her heart-shaped face with rather pouting lips gave her an air of voluptuousness, which was further confirmed by the outline of her figure, clearly visible in its form-fitting dress.

'You're on!' a voice hissed in Caroline's ear, and making her mind a blank, she glided on to the stage.

To the audience it seemed that no one could be cooler than these beautiful young girls as they paraded the exquisite clothes. But backstage it was a different story. Buttons snapped, hooks and eyes refused to meet, and accessories mysteriously vanished. Tempers rose and exploded as the seamstress made last-minute adjustments, frequently sewing the girls into their dresses.

It was near to bedlam as they all came out dressed for the finale. Caroline with her silver-blonde hair was the ideal choice for the bride, and knew that the floating silk organza dress emphasised the subtle curves of her slender figure.

They paraded to 'A Pretty Girl is Like a Melody', and as they took their last turn and came to a halt, Caroline found herself directly in line with the lovely young girl she had been watching earlier. But this time it was the man who caught her attention, for his dark eyes, marked by heavy brows, seemed to be locked on hers with an intensity that sent an electric current through her. She shivered and had the uncomfortable feeling that he was aware of the effect he was having on her. The girl behind nudged her to move, and she turned and sauntered towards the back of the stage, resisting the urge to pick up her skirts and run. Only as she reached the safety of backstage did she breathe a sigh of relief and try to collect her turbulent thoughts.

Who was the man to whom she had been so instantly attracted? It had been mutual, she was sure, because he had been willing her to catch his eyes.

'Don't stand there dreaming,' someone ordered her. 'I've got to pack that wedding dress.'

With a murmured apology Caroline hastily stepped out of it and into her own dress, then methodically began to wipe off her heavy make-up. She was startled as someone touched her shoulder and looked up to see Rick Henderson.

'Lovely show, darling. You make a beautiful bride. You have that virginal glow that convinces one it's the real thing!' He studied her reaction. 'But then perhaps it is?'

'You'll never know!'

'Keep your cool,' he chuckled. 'I'm about to do you a good turn. Having pumped me for information about Matt Bishop—which I was delighted to give you—I'm now going to give you the chance of meeting him.'

Caroline wanted to refuse. Matt Bishop—from all she had learned of him—was the type she preferred to avoid. But since she hoped to be working for one of his companies, it might not be diplomatic to turn down Rick's offer.

As soon as she was ready she made her way into the gilded and mirrored ballroom which the hotel staff were starting to clear. She saw the man standing beside Rick and her heart skipped a beat. It was the same one who had been staring at her during the fashion show. Quickly she recovered her composure and walked forward.

'Matt Bishop—Lady Caroline Haveling,' Rick introduced them. 'The only real "lady" in the business!'

'And certainly one of the loveliest.' Matt Bishop's voice was low, with a hint of a Northern accent. 'I've heard about you from Mark Ingle. I believe he's a friend of your brother's, which means I'm in luck.'

'Luck?' she queried.

'That we have a mutual friend.' His tone was slightly mocking. 'Though as your employer-to-be, I feel our meeting would have happened later if not sooner.'

Some of her pleasure died. If he was the sort of man who used his business position to further his personal interests, she would have to make it plain that she would not play along with him.

'Would you care for a drink?' he cut into her thoughts. 'Or would it be old-fashioned of me to suggest tea?'

'I'm an old-fashioned girl,' she said. 'Tea would be lovely.'

'With bread and butter and jam?'

'Of course. I'm starving. I've only had one coffee and a dried-up sandwich all day.'

'I'm only allowing you a small tea,' he warned. 'I don't want to spoil your appetite for dinner tonight.'

Caroline stiffened. The speed of his progress made her nervous. 'What makes you think I'm having dinner with you tonight?'

'Aren't you?'

'No.' His cool assumption that she would say yes had annoyed her. 'I've had a hard day. Some other time, perhaps?'

'I won't take no for an answer.' He turned to Rick. 'Any time I can do you a good turn, let me know. I owe you one, sport.' Taking Caroline by the arm, he steered her towards the door.

'Are you always such a fast worker, Mr Bishop?' she enquired.

'Matt, please—and yes, I am. If I see what I like I don't believe in waiting for someone else to beat me to it.'

The hotel lounge was fairly full, mainly with foreign visitors, but at one table sat a group of expensively dressed women, among whom was Penny. Sitting next to her was the stunning girl who had been watching the show with Matt Bishop.

'Caroline ... and Matt ... how lovely to see you,' Penny greeted them both. 'I looked for you when I came backstage,' she murmured to her friend, 'But I just missed you.'

While Penny was talking, Caroline was aware of being closely watched by the dark-haired girl, and was in no way surprised when Matt Bishop introduced her as his ward, Helen Warner.

Returning Caroline's warm smile with a cold one, the girl immediately addressed herself to Matt.

'I thought you said you had business to discuss with Rick Henderson?'

'I had,' said Matt.

'Then if it's finished you can take me home.'

'I'm having tea with Lady Caroline.'

'I'll wait.'

'There's no need,' he said easily.

Helen stood up. 'I'll meet you back at the flat. Don't forget you said you were taking me to dinner.'

'You misunderstood me,' he said casually. 'What I said was that we'd have dinner together if I were free. But I won't be.'

Before the girl could protest he caught Caroline's arm and steered her towards a table in the corner, and they sat down.

'I must apologise for Helen,' he said. 'She's inclined to be possessive.'

'Maybe she has a reason,' Caroline said innocently.

'*I* have a reason for condoning her behaviour. I was responsible for her parents' death in a plane crash. Not technically,' he added, 'but morally. They hadn't wanted to fly that day, but I insisted.' He half sighed. 'Since then, Helen's looked on me as her father. She's a good kid, and when you get to know her better you'll like her.'

Caroline doubted it. From what she had learned of Helen, the girl's rudeness stemmed from jealousy, and if Matthew Bishop didn't realise it he must be a fool.

The waitress came over to take their order, and as she set the cups and plates down Caroline had a chance to study Matt. He was physically rugged, with wide shoulders, and had difficulty fitting his long legs under the top of the small table. His hair was almost black, and very thick, worn brushed straight back from his high forehead and worn long at the nape of the neck. His nose, in the slim, lightly tanned face, was rather long—aristocratic-looking, she decided, as was the wide but thin-lipped mouth.

'Do I meet with your approval?' he asked.

She flushed. 'You must think me very rude, staring at you like that, but I'm rather inclined to judge people by first impressions.'

'I hope I'm making a good one!'

'I'm sure you're not worried about my opinion.'

'I always worry about the opinions of a beautiful woman.' He paused as their tea was set before them, and then continued, 'You're the first model I've met with a title.'

'I never use it,' she assured him.

'But you will if you and your brother do this job for Mark? The idea would be pointless without it.'

'I agreed to do it as a favour to my brother.'

'What a wonderful sister you are!'

Caroline knew at once that he had thought she was playing hard to get, but because she did not want to go into any explanations about Tom she silently poured the tea and began to eat. Deliberately she made no conversation, and to her surprise neither did he.

Only when she put a large cream pastry on her plate did he speak.

'Now that you're not as hungry I hope you're in a more responsive mood.'

'I'm always like this,' she said sweetly.

'Have some more sugar, then.'

She couldn't help a smile, and instantly Matt returned it.

'That's better,' he said. 'Now perhaps you'll have dinner with me.'

She laughed. 'Couldn't we make it another night?'

'Of course. But I want to have dinner with you tonight as well!'

Again it was impossible for her to keep a straight face and he took her smile as acquiescence. 'No more pastries,' he warned, 'or you won't be hungry later on.'

'Don't bet on that. I eat like a horse!'

'No calorie counting?'

'Rarely.' She took another bite of her pastry. 'Food —eating as well as cooking it—is one of my hobbies. If there'd been as much money in it as modelling, I'd have taken it up professionally.'

'Surely you don't *need* to work?'

'Having a title doesn't automatically mean you're rich. My parents died when Tom and I were children and we were brought up by my mother's sister and her husband, who are far from wealthy.'

'But aristocratic, I assume?' His tone was faintly mocking.

'You assume wrong.' She said no more and glanced at her watch. 'If you don't want me to look like an old hag, I'd better go home and freshen up.'

With a nod Matt stood up and draped her jacket over her shoulders. His hands brushed against her arm and she was startlingly aware of it.

Hoping he hadn't noticed, she followed him out to a wine-coloured Rolls that was parked in the half moon of the marble and glass entrance. A uniformed chauffeur nipped out smartly and held open the door.

'Will you let me take you home?' Matt asked.

Caroline nodded and gave the chauffeur her address in Hampstead.

'Where do you live?' she asked Matthew Bishop as she settled back in the seat.

'In Regent's Park. It's near my office—which saves time. Time is the most precious thing I have.'

'Yet you came to a fashion show?'

'Because it was business.'

'Business?' she queried.

'I wanted to see if the clothes were suitable for my new venture.'

'And are they?'

'Some of them—yes. I was very impressed.'

'Do you think women will buy such expensive clothes by mail order?'

'No doubt of it—and men too. Lots of people with money are still overwhelmed by smart boutiques and high-pressured salesmanship. Before I decided to go into this, I had some market research done on the subject, and I was amazed by the result. Most wives help to choose their husbands' clothes anyway, and women often like the approval of their husbands before making an expensive purchase. So if they can do it in the comfort of their own home, so much the better.'

Caroline nodded and he went on expanding the subject. He became animated as he talked about his business, and made it so interesting that she was astonished when the car stopped outside her front door.

'I'll collect you at eight,' he said.

'Come up for a drink first,' she invited.

'I'd love to.'

It was only as she entered her flat that she remembered her car was still parked in the hotel garage. What an idiot she was! Meeting Matt Bishop had made her completely forget about it!

CHAPTER TWO

JANE was not in, and a note on the hall table said she was having a farewell dinner with some friends and would not be back until late. Caroline was relieved. She could do without Jane's friendly chatter at this moment. Her reaction to Matt had taken her by surprise, for she was not usually bowled over by the men she met. Yet this one had disturbed her, and she was not sure she liked it.

She ran a bath and luxuriously soaked away her weariness in the warm, scented water, trying to put Matt Bishop out of her mind. She must have dozed off, because when she looked at her watch on the stool beside her, she saw it was nearly seven.

Hurriedly she dried herself and went to inspect her wardrobe. She discarded one dress after another, and after a great deal of deliberation chose a soft green silk jersey that clung to her figure in all the right places. She put her long hair up, then decided it was too severe and let it hang loose, framing her face and making her look younger than her twenty-four years. She was a natural blonde, but unlike most blondes had a warm peachy skin and unusually deep-coloured eyes of a curious grey-green, one or other colour predominating according to what she wore. The rest of her features were small and neat, though the fullness of her lower lip betokened a passionate nature which her calm expression hid. Slender, like most models, she was well curved enough not to appear thin and was frequently propositioned to pose for nude photographs. They were offers she always turned down, though she was well aware that her days as a model would last only as long as her looks remained fashionable.

Going into the sitting-room, she made sure the room was tidy, plumping up the cushions of the sofa and emptying a dirty ashtray. That would be one of the nice things about having the place to herself. Jane was a heavy smoker and this was one of Caroline's pet hates.

Promptly at eight the buzzer went. She pressed the catch for the entryphone, then waited at the top of the stairs to greet Matt as he came striding up the two flights.

'You're very punctual,' she greeted him.

'Since I hate to be kept waiting I always make a point of being on time.'

He followed her into the room and glanced quickly round before seating himself. She could tell from his expression that he was impressed. The room was large and high-ceilinged, as in all old houses, with one end used for dining. A round, glass-topped table with a chrome base was surrounded by six white leather chairs, and a smoked brown glass and chrome wall-fitting containing a bar fitment and some expensive stereo equipment was used as a room divider. The walls were painted deep brown and offset by cream ceiling and skirtings, and the curtains on their Victorian brass rods were in the same orange silk as the sofa. Several antique pieces were dotted around the room, stopping it from having a stark modern look.

As Caroline prepared the whisky and ice Matt had

asked for, she knew he was studying her, and woman-like, she responded to it, moving towards him with exaggerated grace and pushing back her long, streaky blonde hair with a deliberate gesture. The line of her high cheekbones was pure, and she gave him plenty of time to see it before she let her hair swing forward again.

'Aren't you drinking?' he asked.

'Only tomato juice.' She poured herself one and sat opposite him, slowly crossing her long slim legs.

'Does that mean you're teetotal?' he went on.

'Oh no. I like white wine and champagne and leave the hard stuff for the grown-ups!'

His eyes narrowed. 'I'd say you were very grown up.'

She looked at him unblinkingly and he shrugged and glanced around the room.

'I like the way you've done this. You've got some good antiques. Pricey too.'

'Do you judge everything by its cost?' she asked wryly.

'Only horses and women.'

Round one to you, she thought.

'What made you take up modelling?' he asked abruptly.

'Chance. When I left boarding school I wanted to earn my keep as soon as possible, and my uncle helped me get a job with some friends of his. They ran a modelling school, but I was general dogsbody in the office, until one day Lee Lloyd the photographer came in looking for a model to use for a fashion spread. He asked me if I would do some freelance work for him. Later on he introduced me to Penny and from then on I've never looked back.'

'Funny you should know Lee Lloyd so well,' said Matt. 'He's doing the catalogue for me.'

'That's good. We've always worked well together. Some photographers can be real swine.'

'So can Lloyd if the mood takes him, but he's the best there is.' He rose. 'I think we should make a move.'

'I'll just get my shawl.'

She reappeared a moment later with a fringed silk shawl that matched her dress, and followed him down to the car.

'No chauffeur?' she said in surprise.

'I prefer to drive myself when I'm dining with a beautiful girl,' he told her. 'I find it offputting to have Frank discreetly peering in the mirror!' He set the car in motion. 'I've booked a table at the White Elephant.'

'Lovely! It's one of my favourite restaurants.'

From the way Matt was greeted when they arrived there she could see he was a favoured client.

'No propping up the bar tonight,' he told the head waiter. 'My guest prefers food to drink.'

They were led through the pine-panelled restaurant, with its soft lighting, to a corner table at the back of the room, and were handed large, elaborate menus. While they were studying them a bottle of champagne was brought to their table.

'Do they mind-read here?' Caroline questioned.

'They know you're the champagne type,' he said seriously. 'And I know you're the eating type. So let's order.'

The conversation centred on trivialities during the excellent meal, giving Caroline some respite from her emotions. Even the accidental brushing of their hands across the table when Matt passed the salt set her body tingling, and she was pleased to keep things on an impersonal level.

Matt did not hide his surprise at her appetite, not really believing she could eat her way through the rich meal, and when Caroline took a mélange of the rich creamy desserts from the trolley, he laughed openly.

'I thought I was bad enough, but you take the cake!'

'Then why don't you take some!'

'I have to watch my weight.'

'You don't look as if you do,' she said.

'I work out every morning at a gym, and play squash whenever I can. How about you? Indoor or outdoor sports!'

She was irritated at his obviousness and he was quick enough to sense it.

'Sorry,' he said. 'Old habits die hard. But take the question at face value.'

'I don't need to play any sports. My job keeps me thin. It can be pretty exhausting.' She sipped her wine. 'I occasionally play tennis in Regent's Park when I can muster up the energy.'

'I usually walk there at weekends—if I have the time.'

'You work pretty long hours, don't you?' she commented.

'Some days aren't long enough. To stay in this rat race you've got to be one jump ahead of the next guy.'

'You sound cynical,' she remarked.

'I am. I came up the hard way—not via the old school tie network.'

'How did you get started?'

Unlike most self-made men he seemed reluctant to discuss his beginnings and tried to brush her questioning aside.

'It's a long story, and it will bore you.'

'No, it wouldn't. Do tell me.'

Realising she was not just idly curious, he began to talk, and Caroline learned that his father had kept a tiny drapery shop in the poorest part of Bradford.

'Money was always short,' he said, 'and half the customers bought the stuff on tick.'

'Tick?'

'They owed for the goods and paid when they could,' he explained. 'But when work was short they didn't pay at all. My mother helped out by charring at the Town Hall. My parents scrimped and scraped to let me stay on at school and I took all sorts of part-time jobs to earn a few extra quid. Fortunately I was a bright lad and won a place at grammar school.' He leaned over, refilling her wine glass. 'My father wanted me to go to university—I was clever enough—but I wanted to start earning money so that I could help them.' He paused, his expression so reflective that she knew he was deep in his past. When he spoke seriously he was a different person and far nicer than the brash, playboy image he wore at other times. 'Like you, I had a lucky break,' he went on. 'I got a job in a local brewery firm and after I'd been there a year the chairman stopped to talk to me. It was his principle to talk to the highest and lowest, and that day it was my turn. He must have taken a fancy to me, for the next thing I knew, I was promoted to head office and became his protégé. By the time the old boy retired I was running the company, and a few years after that I was chairman. My next step was to diversify. We went into property at the right time, and we used the profits to buy into a dozen other companies.'

'Are you chairman of them all?' she asked.

'I'm chairman of the main board—which is the one that controls all the companies.'

'It's a wonderful success story. You must be very proud of yourself.'

'From rags to riches?'

'In a way. I mean, you began with nothing, didn't you?'

'Only a good éducation,' he said so dryly that she was discomfited.

'I'm sorry if I sounded patronising. I meant it as a compliment.'

'No need to apologise,' he said. 'I'm not as sensitive about it as I was when I was young and broke. My money makes me acceptable in *any* circle now.'

'People are such snobs, aren't they?' she agreed.

'You aren't,' he said.

'How do you know?'

'Because of the way you reacted when you thought you'd hurt me. You're a sensitive young lady, Lady Caroline.'

'Thank you very much, *Mr* Bishop.'

They smiled at one another, and Matt leaned back in his chair.

'You've done well too,' he said. 'According to Rick you're at the top of the tree.'

'Professionally,' she said.

'Socially too. Rick filled me in on your background.'

Caroline was chilled. She did not like the idea of this man questioning Rick about her background, and even less did she like the idea of the lurid way in which Rick might have answered him.

'Don't look so upset.' Matt leaned forward. 'Rick was highly complimentary about you—and I discarded half the scandal he dredged up.'

'Scandal?' She felt herself stiffen.

'About your family. Though personally your father sounded like a hell of a good guy.'

'He was,' Caroline agreed, 'and he and my mother were as much in love on the day they died as when they got married.'

'Then they were lucky people.'

'My grandparents didn't think so.' Caroline was back in her own past. 'They refused to have anything to do with my father from the moment he ran away and married my mother. They had an American heiress lined up for him and they never forgave him for marrying the daughter of a publican.'

Matt chuckled. 'I knew we had something in common.'

'Have we?' She was mystified.

'The brewery business!'

She laughed, and humour helped the hurt of the past to recede so that she could talk about it more easily.

'I never knew my paternal grandparents,' she said. 'They acted as if we never existed. They couldn't prevent my father inheriting the title, but they left all the family money to charity.'

'You're beautiful enough not to need help from anyone,' he said.

'For the moment,' she replied. 'But in this business

there's always someone younger and prettier waiting to step into your shoes.'

'Not for years yet,' he assured her.

She smiled, then glanced at her watch.

'How inconsiderate I am,' said Matt. 'I didn't realise how late it was.'

'Not really, but my flatmate is moving tomorrow and I promised to help her.'

He motioned the waiter for the bill and they made their way through the restaurant. It was still fairly full, even at this late hour, and he stopped at several tables to speak to acquaintances. The men looked admiringly at Caroline, and though she could not overhear their remarks, she realised from the glances they gave her she was being discussed. Knowing Matt's reputation with women, she could imagine what they were saying, and because she had enjoyed her evening she found herself hoping he would not spoil it by making the obligatory pass.

During the drive home she was tense, and when the car drew up outside her front door, she quickly fumbled at the lock.

'Aren't you going to ask me in for a nightcap?' he said.

'You shouldn't drink and drive,' she replied sweetly.

'By the time I leave, the effects will have worn off.'

Disappointment washed over her, and angrily she jumped out.

'If you want me to pay for my evening, I'd rather do it with money!' she snapped.

He was halfway round the side of the car and he stopped.

'Ouch,' he said slowly, 'that was a right to the chin.'.

'I'm sorry. But if you assume that one date entitles you to spend the night with me, I'm afraid you've wasted your time and money. And I know how precious both of those things are to you!'

'And that was below the belt!' Anger deepened his voice and his Northern accent was more pronounced. 'I don't need to force myself on any girl.'

'You could have fooled me!'

'Perhaps you're the one who's doing the fooling.' He was beside her, looming tall. 'Are you really as outraged as you profess? You've been around long enough to know the score.'

'And you've been around long enough to know when a girl doesn't want to play!'

'In general, or just with me?'

'In general,' she said icily.

'Saving yourself for the man you marry?' he asked sarcastically.

'How clever of you to guess.'

She was at the top of the steps and had inserted the key in the lock before he was aware of it.

'Caroline!' he called.

'Goodnight!,' she replied, and slammed the door in his face.

So much for her hopes that he would behave differently with her from the way he normally did. He was an arrogant boor and she never wanted to see him again. If it weren't for Tom she'd refuse to do the modelling assignment. Shivering, she let herself into the flat. Even though she had to work for one of Matthew Bishop's companies she had no intention of having anything to do with its owner.

CHAPTER THREE

JANE ran Caroline back to the Berkeley Hotel first thing the next morning to collect her car. Arriving back, they found the removal men waiting for them as well as an enormous basket of pink and white roses. Caroline read the simple message on the card that was nestling among the tightly closed buds.

'Please forgive me. Will you let me make amends at dinner tonight?'

Fuming at his audacity, Caroline expended her angry energy on helping Jane. She tried to put Matt out of her mind, but the flowers kept reminding her of him, and at nine o'clock when the telephone rang she knew he was at the other end of the line.

'If it's Matthew Bishop I'm not in,' she told Jane.

'Like that, eh?' Jane replied, and in gentle tones informed Mr Bishop that the object of his call was unavailable.

Exactly an hour later another bouquet arrived, twice as large as the first one. There was no message this time.

'You'll be able to open your own florist's shop,' Jane commented. 'What did he do last night, for God's sake?'

'Nothing, and he's not going to get another chance tonight. If he ...'

The peal of the telephone interrupted her, and Caroline motioned her friend again to answer it.

'No, Mr Bishop,' said Jane, 'Lady Caroline is still unavailable.'

An hour later another gift arrived. Not flowers this time but a beautiful Hermès scarf.

'I'd like to strangle him with it!' Caroline snapped, and flung it on the sofa.

No telephone call followed the arrival of this gift, but an hour later another package arrived; an outrageously expensive flagon of the finest French perfume.

'It still won't make that rat smell any sweeter,' Caroline fumed, and handed it to Jane. 'Use it to bowl Bruce over.'

'I wonder what you'll get next,' grinned Jane. 'I can see this going on all day.'

'He'll have to give up some time,' Caroline shrugged. 'Meanwhile I'll start filling your bottom drawer for you.'

'I wish he knew what size tights I wore,' Jane chuckled.

But the next gift that arrived came at lunch time, and was a lavish hamper from Fortnum's, filled with home-made pâté, a creamy asparagus quiche, hot-house Muscatel grapes and peaches, and a bottle of champagne. This time there was a message with it too, written in the same handwriting as the card that had accompanied the flowers.

'I know you're always a crosspatch until you eat, so I'll wait for the second burp and call you!'

'You really should talk to him,' Jane counselled, her plain face pink with the excitement of it all.

'You're too softhearted,' Caroline snapped. 'It's time

Matthew Bishop learned he can't have every girl he fancies.'

'Do you fancy him?' asked Jane.

'Yes. But that's as far as it will go.'

'We're two old-fashioned girls,' Jane muttered. 'Isn't it a shame!'

Matt's call came at three o'clock, and Jane was almost apologetic as she repeated the lie she had uttered twice already. This time when she put down the telephone she looked woebegone.

'He sounded furious!' she exclaimed.

'Good. That should be the last we'll hear of him.'

But she was proved wrong, for at four o'clock a vast box of chocolates, almost two feet square, was delivered to her door by Matt's chauffeur, Frank.

'How's this for a sweetener?' Matt had penned.

'Could you drop the box into Great Ormond Street Hospital on your way back?' Caroline asked Frank.

'Very good, my lady,' he said, poker-faced, and carrying the box nipped smartly down the stairs.

An hour later, with both Caroline and Jane waiting expectantly for a ring at the door bell, there was nothing.

'He's finally taken the hint,' said Jane.

'Thank heavens for that,' Caroline lied, and felt her heart give a lurch as the bell vibrated sharply in her ear. This time she was at the door before Jane, and once more saw Frank. Silently he held out a small package and stood impassively while she opened it. Inside was a jewellery box, and nestling on a bed of black satin, a gold charm. It was a dog kennel, containing a miniature poodle with tiny emerald eyes peeping up at her.

'There's a note with it, my lady,' the chauffeur said, and handed it to her.

'Haven't I been in the doghouse long enough?' she read. Her lips twitched, and she burst out laughing. She was still laughing when the telephone rang, and this time she answered it herself.

'Are you willing to share a bone with me tonight?' Matt asked, 'and afterwards you can bang it on my head.'

'What a lovely idea!'

'I knew you'd think so. I'll call for you at eight-thirty.'

'You must let me know what happens,' said Jane, coming out of the bedroom as Caroline put down the telephone. 'It's just my luck to move out at a time like this.'

'I hope I've shown Matt Bishop that it's not his luck,' Caroline said as she kissed her friend goodbye, and tried not to feel regret that Jane was finally leaving. She would miss her companionship, but would soon appreciate having the flat to herself.

She tried to feel calm about the evening ahead, but as it drew near she could not stop the excitement mounting in her. Be careful, she warned herself. The fact that Matt apologised doesn't mean he won't try again.

To prove to herself that he was unimportant to her she dressed casually in a pink cashmere two-piece, and settled herself on the couch to wait. In a few minutes she was fast asleep.

She was awakened by the blasting of a horn, and hurried to the window to see Matt's car below. He was

on time again. She ran down the steps and he greeted
her with a smile.

He was dressed casually too, in a light grey suit and
a blue shirt. His eyes were glinting with humour and
for the first time she noticed the colour; brown with
gold flecks in them. He had short lashes, but they were
thick like his hair.

'I decided not to risk coming up to call for you,' he
said.

'Is that an admission of defeat or good tactics?'

'Both. I believe in biding my time.'

'You didn't bide it very long last night.'

'More fool me,' he said. 'But you're so beautiful you
made me lose my head.'

Caroline did not believe that a man of his experience
could not control himself, and knew he was mouthing
words he did not mean. He wanted her, and had not
seen any reason to pretend otherwise. But now he had
learned his lesson and would be wary how he treated
her.

'You'd better have hot milk tonight instead of champagne. It will cool your ardour,' she said.

'I'll keep off oysters too,' he shot her a quick glance.
'I thought we'd go to Maidenhead. I know a wonderful
place on the river.'

'As long as you don't give me a reason to push you
in!'

'Don't you trust me?' he asked plaintively, and
without waiting for an answer set the car in motion.

The restaurant he took her to was in a beautiful
old-world mansion, and the food was excellent. As if
realising Caroline had worked hard all day, Matt re-

galed her with amusing stories that required no response, enabling her to enjoy the delicious menu he had ordered for her.

'The only thing I didn't choose was your dessert,' he said, as the main course plates were cleared away. 'I was frightened of picking something too plain!'

She nodded seriously and studied the dessert menu. 'What is Charlotte Malakoff aux Fraises?' she asked.

The waiter kissed the tips of his fingers. 'Layers of almond cream, liqueur-filled sponge and fresh strawberries accompanied by Chantilly cream.'

'That's for me!'

Matt eyed her with amusement. 'You're incredible! It must be your appetite that I like most about you!'

'Can't I tempt you to a little?' she asked.

'A little of what?'

'Layers of almond cream, liqueur-filled sponge and fresh strawberries accompanied by Chantilly cream!'

His laugh was spontaneous. 'You're never short of an answer, are you?' she asked.

'Not to that particular question. I'm asked it too many times.'

'Do you always give the same answer?'

'I promise not to repeat myself, then,' he said.

'I bet you don't mean that?'

'You bet right!'

'You play so hard, I'm surprised you find time to do any work.'

'By managing to combine the two.' He smiled at her expression. 'For example, I'll be joining you and your brother when you go down to France. This kind of mail order is a new venture and I want to supervise it myself until it gets off the ground.'

Caroline's heart seemed to skip a beat, and she was not sure whether to be pleased or sorry.

'I can't ever imagine you delegating your work.'

'I assure you I do—otherwise I'd never get time to play!'

She looked past him. 'Here comes my five thousand calories,' she said, and picked up her spoon.

'Do you mind if I smoke a cigar?' asked Matt, when she had finished eating.

'Not at all. I love the smell.'

'You're a girl with no vices,' he sighed. 'You don't drink, you don't smoke, and you don't ...' He smiled. 'Well, we won't go into that again! How come a girl like you hasn't been snapped up by now?'

'I could ask the same question?'

'A wife happens to be one of the things I can do without, although the gossip columnists are always too eager to marry me off.'

'I don't read the gossip columns much,' Caroline shrugged.

'Not interested in how the other half lives?' He paused. 'But I'm forgetting—you *are* the other half!'

'Don't remind me,' she responded. 'I've been trying to live it down for years!'

'Does your brother feel as you do?'

'No. He enjoys his title. It works wonders at impressing the girls.'

'Are you close to him?' asked Matt.

'Yes. Being orphaned when we were young has drawn us together.'

'I envy you. I was an only child, so I had no one to confide in.'

'I don't confide in Tom,' she said. 'It's usually the

other way around. Although he's two years older than
me, I'm the one he's leaned on. I suppose I'm partly
to blame because I've allowed it and so have my aunt
and uncle. He can charm the bubbles out of a glass of
champagne when he chooses.'

'And you have enough effervescence to put them
back again!'

She was pleased by the unusual compliment. 'What
a nice thing to say!'

'I could say a lot of other nice things,' he assured
her.

'I'm more interested in hearing about you.'

'I've already told you my life story.'

'Then tell me how you see your future?'

'As more of the same.'

'And definitely no marriage?'

'Definitely.' The answer was firm and the look on
his face told her that he was not talking for effect but
because he meant it.

'Am I boring you?' he asked.

She was startled. 'Why?'

'Because you just gave a deep sigh.'

'I'm tired,' she admitted.

'What a wife you'd make!'

She giggled. 'The psychological headache? I really
am tired, though. I've been helping Jane to pack, and
it's beginning to catch up on me.'

'You and your not so subtle hints!' Matt smiled. 'I'll
get the bill.'

They drove back leisurely through the dark country
lanes until they reached the motorway, then Matt put
his foot hard down on the accelerator.

'Aren't you afraid of being booked?' Caroline asked, watching the speedometer touch ninety.

'Yes, but there's no point having a car like this if you can't let her go flat out once in a while. Does it worry you, my driving so fast?'

'No. I'm too frightened myself to go at more than fifty, but I like being driven at speed.'

'So you've finally admitted you're a fast girl.'

'Only in a car.'

'Great. I'll find a layby.' Matt made to slow down and feeling her tense up, he chuckled. 'You must mind what you say to me, Caroline.'

'I will,' she said with such fervour that he chuckled again.

'Will you get someone to take Jane's place?' he continued.

'Not now I can afford the rent on my own. It will be nice entertaining friends without worrying about disturbing anyone else.'

'No bumping into boy-friends taking morning tea in the kitchen?'

'I don't spend the night with men at my flat. Nor did Jane,' she answered frigidly. 'So if you're fishing for an invitation again, you're wasting your time.'

'I find it unbelievable that someone as beautiful as you——'

'Perhaps it's because I am so beautiful that I can afford to hold out for marriage,' she interrupted coolly. 'Don't keep trying with me. I meant what I said before. I don't play around.'

'How do you know I'm playing?' he replied, and with a sudden swerve drew off the road into a layby.

Leaning over, he roughly pulled her into his arms, his mouth fastening on hers, warm and demanding. In spite of her anger she could not stop her instinctive response, and aroused by it, he became more ardent, and he tried to part her lips.

She wrenched away from him. 'No, Matt.'

'You're a girl with a whim of iron.' Lightly he kissed her mouth. 'But iron can rust if left too long. So be warned!'

They started to drive again and went some miles before he spoke. 'Are you free to see me on Saturday?'

'Do you want to?'

'I told you I never give up.'

'I find it rather boring to have to keep saying no,' she sighed.

'I won't keep asking you,' he promised. 'I'll just keep sipping hot milk and feeling miserable!'

She laughed. 'I'm only going out with you because I like your sense of humour.'

'I don't care what the reason is.' He caught hold of her hand and squeezed it. 'Saturday, then?'

'I was going down to my aunt's for the weekend.'

'I'm glad you used the past tense. And keep Sunday free too.'

'Do you always give your girl-friends such a rush?' Caroline asked drily.

'Always.'

It was not quite the answer she wanted, but it reminded her not to take him seriously. It would be all too easy to fall for him. Unaccountably, she thought of Helen Warner and knew the girl could be an implacable enemy. She might be Mark's fiancée, but she saw herself as Matt Bishop's wife.

Idly she watched him as he drove, liking his command of the car, and knowing he would not be happy until he was commanding her in the same way. He wanted her to be Trilby to his Svengali, and she hoped she had the strength to retain a will of her own!

CHAPTER FOUR

CAROLINE slept fitfully, her mind too active for sound sleep, and the alarm clock awakened her too early to feel refreshed.

Penny telephoned her to fill her in on the arrangements for her trip to France, saying that she and Tom were to fly down with Lee Lloyd the photographer, who was also taking his fiancée.

'Fiancée?' Caroline queried.

'She's his assistant as well. You've all been booked in to the Hotel Riviera. It's a few miles from Antibes. You're getting the de luxe treatment, old girl. My ex and I spent a long weekend there before we married, when he was trying to impress me with his money!'

Caroline wondered if Matt were trying to do the same. 'How long will we be away?'

'About ten days. By the way, how are you getting on with Matt? Still seeing him?'

'Yes. We went to Maidenhead for dinner last night.'

'Take care you don't fall for him,' warned Penny. 'He has a reputation for lovin' and leavin'.'

'Yes, Mum!'

Penny laughed. 'I'm only warning you. You're the type that takes things to heart, and I don't want you to get hurt.'

'We're just good friends,' Caroline assured her.

'I've heard that one before!'

Penny rang off and Caroline was left to think over her warning.

The next few weeks flew by. Matt occupied all her free time, taking her out to expensive restaurants and clubs. He was a knowledgeable and amusing companion, and though absorbed in his business he took an interest in many other things. He knew far more about art and classical music than she did and they spent several Sundays browsing round the galleries or attending concerts at the Festival Hall. He rarely spoke to her about his work, as if frightened of boring her, but questioned her often about her own.

He also enjoyed a childish prank, as she learned one evening when they were out to dinner. An old school friend spotted her and came over with her husband. When she introduced them to Matt it was obvious from their expressions that they recognised his name and were very impressed. He responded to their plummy effusions by speaking with an almost incomprehensible Yorkshire accent, and kept a straight face as he observed their bemused looks when they tried to understand him. Immediately they were out of earshot he burst into laughter, and Caroline couldn't help joining in.

'Why did you speak that way?' she asked.

'I only spoke in the way they expected me to.'

'I don't think they expected it at all,' she protested. 'You're too conscious of your background, Matt. England's not a class-ridden society any more.'

'That's what you think.'

She recognised his tone and did not argue with him.

He was silent for several moments, then leaned over and lightly touched her hand.

'You're a nice girl, Caroline, and clever too.'

'Why do you say that?' She was surprised by the compliment, for although he paid her many they had all been physical ones.

'Because you know when not to argue with me. If more women had that sort of sensitivity, there'd be fewer unhappy marriages.'

'I'll remember that.'

'I'll bet you will!'

On Saturday he telephoned her early and told her to fish out her passport and be ready in half an hour. Giving her no time to question him, he rang off.

They drove to London Airport and boarded a Paris plane. On arrival, a chauffeur-driven car awaited them, and they toured the city, rounding off a glorious day with dinner at Maxim's.

Since first kissing her, he had behaved with complete propriety, keeping his emotions so well checked that Caroline began to wonder at his restraint. Deciding to give him some encouragement, and show him that she trusted him now, she invited him to her flat for dinner the following night.

'About time too,' he said. 'You've boasted so much about your cooking, I was beginning to wonder if it was a myth.'

He arrived carrying a bottle of Dom Perignon champagne and a large bunch of roses. 'I thought we'd celebrate our anniversary,' he said as he kissed her.

'Anniversary?' she queried.

'We've known each other five weeks and I've not had my evil way with you once!'

'Is that a record?'

'One I shouldn't like to play too often!'

'Give me the champagne,' she said quickly. 'I'll put it in the refrigerator.'

'There's no need. It's already cold. I've been keeping it on ice.'

'I have the feeling you've been doing the same thing with me for the past few weeks! I hope you don't expect me to melt tonight.'

'What a suspicious mind you have,' he replied, and filled their glasses. 'Haven't I behaved like a gentleman?'

'Perhaps that's because you know I'm a lady!' Caroline said demurely as they took their glasses over to the dining table.

The meal she had prepared was so good that even Matt, with his fastidious palate, was impressed, particularly with the coq au vin and her wafer-thin crêpes Suzettes brought flaming to the table.

Afterwards they sat relaxed on the settee, Matt sipping his brandy and Caroline her black coffee. She had refused his offer to help with the dishes.

'I'm rather glad you did,' he confessed. 'I'm all fingers and thumbs when it comes to domestic chores. Always have been.'

'I didn't think you were the type of bachelor who'd spent much time in the kitchen.'

'The bedroom is more my line,' he agreed, edging closer to her.

'Would you like some coffee?' she asked hastily.

'No, thanks, I'd much rather have you,' he said huskily, and pulling her into his arms gently pressed her down on the couch. His mouth fastened on hers, its pressure intensifying as he felt her respond, while his hands gently massaged her breasts. His touch awakened her desire and set her body alight, and she became increasingly aware of the urgency in him as his body lay tightly pressed against her own. She felt as if she were drowning in his hold, and the sensual endearments he murmured—combined with the movements of his hand as he expertly started to undo the zip of her dress—made her realise that unless she resisted him now she would be lost. Pushing him away, she sat up.

'Why did you stop me?' he asked, his voice low. 'You know you want me as much as I want you.'

'Maybe, but that doesn't alter my principles.'

'For God's sake,' he said irritably. 'We've known each other for five weeks.'

'I'd feel the same if it were five years.' She studied his face. 'I rather hoped you realised that—or are all women fair game to you?'

'Why shouldn't they be?'

'Because you're old enough to have more sense.'

'Peter Pan's my middle name,' he shrugged.

'Well, mine isn't Wendy,' she said tartly.

He looked so sceptical that her annoyance increased. 'Haven't you *ever* been in love, Matt?' she asked.

'How do you define love?'

'As respect and trust. Desire too, of course.'

'I had respect for a woman once,' he said.

'If it's left you feeling so bitter you must have loved her very much.'

'Enough to marry her.'

The reply was so unexpected, it was difficult to keep the shock out of her face. Yet what she felt was more than shock; it was bitter disappointment too.

'I didn't realise you were married.'

'Was,' he corrected. 'I've been divorced for thirteen years.'

'I'm sorry,' she said softly, and tried to hide her relief.

'I'm not,' he retorted. 'She was a scheming bitch!'

His voice was hard and Caroline could see he was angry. Not wanting to arouse his memories by questioning him further, she remained silent, although she longed to hear the whole story.

'Thanks for controlling your curiosity,' he said unexpectedly. 'But I'll willingly answer any questions.'

'Does it still hurt you to speak about her?'

'No. But I won't let myself get hurt again.' He took out a cheroot, lit it and dragged at it hungrily. 'When I think what a fool I was ...'

'You were young,' Caroline placated.

'I was more than young, I was naïve and idealistic. I was twenty-two when I met Sarah. It was at a party given by Harold Maitland, my boss. I was flattered as hell to be invited. For a boy from the slums of Bradford this was really living, and when Sarah started to chat me up, I couldn't believe my luck. She was the prettiest girl in the room and she made it clear that she fancied me.' He stopped momentarily and pulled at his cheroot. 'Six weeks later I asked her to marry me, and I couldn't believe it when she said yes. What was more surprising was the way her family welcomed me, though a few days after we were married I learned the reason why.'

He paused again as though he found it difficult to carry on, and Caroline was sure he was reliving the hurt of his past. A hurt that was still close to him, no matter what he said to the contrary.

'Sarah told me she was three months pregnant,' he said flatly, 'and she didn't even know whose child it was!'

'You mean——'

'That she was anybody's for the asking! All her friends and family knew it, that's why she picked *me* out!'

'Why hadn't she had an abortion? With money—even in those days—it would have been possible.'

'Because of her religion. Her conscience wouldn't allow it—though it didn't stop her making a damn fool of me!'

'What did you do?' Caroline asked.

'Left her to spend her honeymoon alone,' he stated matter-of-factly. 'Sarah never believed I could do it. Her father was a close friend of Harold Maitland and she was certain I wouldn't want to jeopardise my career. That was her first mistake. Her second one was trying to pretend I was the father of her child.' He stopped for a moment, his face taking on a haunted look. 'I spent every penny I'd saved to get the best divorce lawyer I could. Her name was dirt when I got through with her, and she learned that no one plays me for a fool and gets away with it.'

Caroline did not like the raw hatred in his voice, although she could understand it. It reminded her of the ruthlessness in him which, hidden by charm when he was with her, none the less lay just below the surface.

'It all happened a long time ago,' she murmured. 'You shouldn't let it sour the rest of your life.'

'I haven't. But I refuse to be taken in by innocence again.'

'I'm not trying to take you in, Matt,' Caroline said bluntly. 'And the way I feel about certain things is not an act. If you don't believe me, we shouldn't see each other any more.'

'Of course I believe you. But I also believe I can make you change your mind. You've led the life of a nun for so long that you've got into the habit!' He paused. 'I'd like you to come down to the country with me for the weekend if you're free. Don't worry,' he reassured her, 'we'll be well chaperoned by Helen and Mark.'

Caroline hesitated. The last time she had seen Mark was two years ago, and she was still not sure she wanted to see him socially. What would Matt say if he knew she had once hoped to marry the man who was engaged to his ward?

But she was over him now, and it was foolish to let him affect her decision about accepting Matt's invitation. Matt. She looked at him quickly, as always affected by the sensual curve of his mouth and the determination of his chin. He was a man of strong will, and she shivered at the thought of having him weak in her arms. Yet before that happened, *she* would have to be the weaker, and if she were ...

'Well,' he said, breaking into her thoughts, 'are you free or not? I'm going up tomorrow—about six.'

'I'd like that.' She rose. 'Until tomorrow, then.'

Taking the hint, Matt stood up too. 'Don't forget to bring a bikini—and your chastity belt!'

Tidying up the sitting-room after he had gone, Caroline reflected over all she had learned about Matt.

After the unhappy experience of his marriage it was not to be wondered at that he was cynical. Obviously he was wary of women, seeing them as schemers out to catch him and marry him—as she was!

Caroline stopped dead in the centre of the room. It was the first time she had admitted how deeply she had become involved with Matt. I love that arrogant, self-centred bastard, and I'm pretty sure he loves me, she thought. But how can I get him to admit it? She frowned. To make Matt admit it might not be so difficult, but to get him to ask her to marry him was the problem.

The following evening when he came to collect her, Helen and Mark were in the car. Helen managed a frosty smile, but Mark's greeting was warm and friendly.

'It's nice to see you after all this time,' he said. 'You're looking prettier than ever. I seem to see your face on every magazine cover and hoarding.'

'Not quite every one. I only wish it were.' Caroline took her place beside Matt, delighted that the sight of Mark left her totally unmoved. It was salutary to remember how deeply she had thought herself in love with him. With hindsight she knew she had been too young to know her own mind. With Matt it was different. In five weeks he had become part of her life, and she hoped he would never walk out of it.

The three of them chatted amiably on the drive down to Berkshire, Helen remaining silent. She was obviously annoyed that Caroline was coming with them, and made no effort to hide her feelings.

Matt's house was larger than Mark's had been, and infinitely nicer. Georgian in style and graciously pro-

portioned, it stood in about four acres of gardens, the
rest of the land being run as a farm. They walked under
arched porticoes into the main hall where the floor was
tiled in black and white marble squares, and a beautiful arrangement of summer flowers stood on the green
marble top of a large gold ormolu table. The heady
scent of the flowers filled the air, as Matt proudly
showed her the main reception rooms that ran along
the back of the house and overlooked the terrace and
gardens. She noticed several valuable paintings, though
he did not point them out. He might be naïve in wanting to show off his lovely house, but he was too intelligent to make any comment on his art collection.

But leading her up the galleried staircase, he pointed
to some imposing portraits.

'My ancestors!' he said solemnly.

'All of them?' she asked equally solemnly.

'Of course.' He grinned. 'I bought them with the
house, though you'd be surprised at the number of
folk who actually believe they're my relations!'

'If you married me,' she pointed out sweetly, 'they
might well be!'

'That's too high a price to pay,' he chuckled, and
Helen who was standing behind them pursed her lips
and stalked past them up the stairs.

Matt appeared not to notice his ward's behaviour, or
if he did, he ignored it indulgently. But Caroline was
very aware of her dislike, and this was in no way dis-
pelled during the rest of the weekend.

Her bedroom was as well appointed as any luxury
hotel, the pièce de résistance being a fourposter bed
covered in the same flowery fabric as the curtains. The
en-suite bathroom also contained three different bottles

of expensive scent, a hairdryer and a telephone in
arm's reach of the sunken bath. Caroline was not at all
surprised to find slightly perfumed soapy water running out of the gold-plated taps. Guests had no need to
even trouble themselves about washing in anything as
mundane as a bar of soap!

After changing into a long black skirt and white
satin shirtwaister blouse, she made her way down to
the drawing-room where the rest of the party were
gathered for pre-dinner drinks. She accepted the
tomato juice that Matt poured for her, and seated herself on a wing chair.

'That's a bit unsociable,' Helen remarked, noticing
Caroline had no alcohol added to her drink.

'Caroline only likes champagne,' Matt explained.

'Expensive taste, Caroline,' Helen commented.

'Not if one has rich boy-friends,' Caroline said
sweetly.

'Caroline's never been short of those,' Mark inter-
posed hastily.

'Did you two go out for long?' Matt asked.

'They were nearly engaged,' Helen informed him,
then looked at Caroline. 'I've never been told why you
broke up. Mark is very discreet about his past affairs.'

'It was never an affair,' Caroline said firmly. 'We
were only friends.'

'You don't need to worry, darling,' Mark said to his
fiancée. 'Caroline was always a career girl.'

Caroline longed to deny it, but diplomatically said
nothing. She glanced at Matt, and saw he was frown-
ing. She wondered if he was jealous, and hoped he was.

'Let's have dinner,' he said, pulling Caroline to her
feet.

They ate an excellent meal, served by the house-keeper's daughter, Grace, who with her mother, Mrs Gordon, was the only resident staff kept at the house, extra help coming in on a daily basis. Fortunately most of the conversation centred round the forthcoming trip to France, and Caroline learned that Helen would be joining them too.

'She can't bear to let me out of her sight,' Mark joked, 'but if she'd only set the date for our wedding she wouldn't have to worry about my running off with someone else!'

'Nonsense,' Helen replied shortly. 'Who's heard of an errant fiancé? It's only when they become husbands that one starts to worry!'

'See what I'm up against,' said Mark, looking at Matt.

'It's not my fault,' Matt said. 'I keep telling her to marry you, but she thinks I'm incapable of managing without her.'

'Then find a replacement for her,' Mark suggested.

'I'm working on it.'

Helen snorted. 'Most of the women you go around with wouldn't have the faintest idea of how to manage you.'

'You're a treasure,' Matt agreed. 'But your obligation is to Mark.'

'Here, here!' chided Mark. 'So what about naming the day, Helen?'

'I'll think about it,' she replied, and pushed back her chair. 'Let's have coffee in the drawing-room.'

No sooner were they settled when Matt put on some tapes, and the melodious voice of Ella Fitzgerald soon persuaded them to dance. Matt held Caroline firmly round the waist as he guided her round the room.

'You do something to me,' he said, echoing the words of the song, but she knew what he was referring to. She saw Helen watching them and pulled slightly away. There was something in the girl's cold glances that disquietened her, spoiling what could otherwise have been a perfect evening.

'I hope you don't mind if I have an early night?' she asked.

'I do. But if it means you'll be fighting fit tomorrow ...' His lips nibbled her ear. 'I never like to take advantage of a woman unless she's in prime condition!'

'I get the impression you're not particular what lambs you lead to the slaughter!'

'How wrong you are—I choose them with great care. So don't count sheep before you fall asleep tonight!'

Caroline was still chuckling as she prepared for bed, though Matt's comment confirmed her opinion that he was still too much in command of his emotions to let them take hold of him.

She woke early to find the sun blazing, and donning a bikini under her sundress, went down to the pool that glinted like an aquamarine some hundred yards from the house. Matt was already there, and she felt a rush of tenderness for him as he strode over to greet her. In brief trunks he looked even more virile than she had imagined, the muscles rippling across his chest and his legs firm and strong.

'We're the early birds, it seems,' he said, kissing her lips lightly.

She wriggled away from his hold. 'You're not going to catch your worm yet! Go in the pool and cool off.'

'Yes, my lady!'

He dived into the water, then surfaced. 'Aren't you coming in?'

Caroline nodded, and did so, climbing down the steps.

'Don't you dive?' he asked.

'Not any more. I slipped a disc a few years ago and I have to be careful.'

It was eleven o'clock when Mark and Helen joined them. The girl wore a minuscule bikini that showed off her rather full figure. Sourly she eyed Caroline's slim one, though it did not deter her from tucking into the lunch Mrs Gordon served them on the terrace.

'I suppose you have to diet because of your job?' Helen asked Caroline.

Matt burst out laughing. 'She only does so between meals. I've never known a girl eat so much.' He leaned across and stroked the satiny skin of her shoulder. 'It's a good thing we're being watched,' he whispered. 'But next time I'm going to invite you here on your own.'

Caroline didn't rise to the bait, still determined she was going to be one fish he didn't hook.

The afternoon and the next day passed quickly. The weather held and they swam late on Sunday afternoon for the last time. Then Caroline packed her things and went down to the kitchen to thank Mrs Gordon for her wonderful meals.

'It was a pleasure to cook for you, my lady. If you come again just let me know if there's anything special you'd like.'

'I will,' Caroline promised. 'But perhaps you can tell me if there's anything special Mr Bishop likes.'

'He's pretty easy, really, except for his allergy.'

'His allergy?'

'He can't eat chervil. I happen to know about it because I used it once in a casserole. It was soon after I started working here. I thought I'd get the sack for sure. Poor Mr Bishop! He was in bed for three days. They had to keep him under sedation to stop the itching, and until the swelling went down.'

She gossiped on for several minutes, and only stopped when she heard Caroline's name being called. It was Matt, and Caroline hurried into the hall.

'I'm just going to change,' he informed her. 'I won't be long.'

'Don't worry about me. I'll browse through some magazines.'

She went into the study and picked up the latest copy of *Country Life*. As she did so Helen came in.

'Oh, here you are. I wanted a word with you,' the girl said. 'You need to be put straight on a few things.'

'About our trip to France?' Caroline replied, deliberately misinterpreting her.

'About Matt,' Helen said irritably. 'Don't read too much into this weekend. He won't marry you, you know.'

'Thanks for telling me!'

'It's for your own good.' Helen's dark eyes were hard. 'He was married before, and it left such a scar that he'll *never* marry again. I wouldn't be telling you now if I didn't think it wiser for you to know. I've broken my word by——'

'Don't worry about it,' Caroline interrupted. 'Matt's already told me the story.'

Helen looked so surprised that Caroline wanted to laugh, then with an angry murmur the girl ran out of the room. Caroline tried to see her dislike as a good omen; only the fear that Matt might be falling in love would have provoked Helen into such an indiscretion.

They reached London at midnight. Helen barely spoke during the journey, though as usual Matt appeared not to notice her uncivil behaviour. Caroline hoped this was not a foretaste of what their stay in France was going to be like, but decided not to mention it to Matt. Guilt at having piloted the plane that had killed Helen's parents must still cause him to turn a blind eye to her tantrums.

Matt escorted her to the front door of her flat. 'I'm tied up tomorrow night,' he said. 'But I hope you're free on Tuesday?'

She immediately wondered what he was doing on Monday, but knew better than to ask him. What she didn't know was whether to make herself available on Tuesday.

'I'll be working late myself on Tuesday,' she murmured.

'I'd like to see you, even if it's only for an hour. Phone me as soon as you're free.'

She did so, and he came over to the flat at nine-thirty, took her to a quiet restaurant and brought her home before midnight. Sensing her tiredness, he hugged her close and made no attempt to do more.

'I like you in this mood,' he said. 'There's no fight in you. I'm not afraid of getting a clip to the jaw!'

'But you're not taking advantage of it.'

'I'm a gentleman fighter.' He unlocked the door for her and pushed her through it. 'Go in quickly before I change my mind.'

Caroline's feeling of contentment was shattered by

her brother, who came to see her on Thursday morning. She had not seen much of him during the past few
weeks, though they had spoken on the phone, and he
knew she was seeing Matt.

'I can't stay and talk,' she said. 'I'm due at *Vogue* in
an hour.'

'So you'll be a few minutes late. I have to talk to
you.'

'What have you done?' she asked fearfully, hearing
the urgency in his voice.

'I borrowed some money from Uncle Bill for a business venture. When it fell through I didn't give him
the money back.' Tom nibbled at his lip. 'I started
gambling with it and lost the lot.'

Caroline looked at her brother with distaste. Joan
and Bill Coleman had acted as surrogate parents to
them from the moment their own had died. They had
given them a far more expensive education than they
could afford, even though it had meant considerable
financial sacrifices to them. In recent years Uncle Bill
had amassed a small amount of money, and it was dis-
gusting of Tom to take advantage of it.

'How much did you borrow?' she asked.

'Ten thousand pounds.'

Disbelief held her spellbound, but only for a
moment. Then anger washed over her. 'I suggest you
try the Mint,' she said furiously. '*I* can't help you.'

'You've got to! I'm desperate.'

'Where can I get that kind of money? If you think
I'm going to ask Matt ...'

'You won't need to. All you have to do is agree to
marry him when he asks you.'

'Agree to ... What are you talking about, Tom?'

'I'm talking about what Mark told me. He says Bishop is going to propose to you when you're in Antibes. Apparently Helen's worried sick.'

'But how will this help you?' she asked, mystified.

'If you sign an agreement saying you'll accept Bishop's proposal and stay engaged to him for three months, Mark will give me the money to pay back Uncle Bill.'

'Mark?' Caroline was still puzzled. 'Why should *he* help you?'

'Because he wants to marry Helen, and he has no hope of doing so while Matt is still single. Helen is only using Mark to try and make Matt jealous, and Mark knows it.'

'And he's willing to give you ten thousand pounds on the chance that if I marry Matt, Helen will marry *him*?'

'Yes.'

'He must love her very much,' said Caroline drily.

'Love has nothing to do with it.' Tom's grey-green eyes, so like his sister's, were bleak. 'When Matt bought Mark's family business he gave Helen a hefty whack of the shares and Mark would like to get his hands on them. If he did he would then have control of the company again.'

'That wouldn't make Matt very happy.'

'Matt couldn't care less. When he gave Helen the shares she was already engaged to Mark. So he must have had some idea of what would happen to them if they married. But with Helen refusing to name the day, Mark's getting increasingly impatient, and he's convinced she'll never do so till Matt is hooked. That's why he's willing to pay you ten thousand pounds to say yes when Matt proposes to you.'

Caroline started to giggle, then the giggle became a chuckle and suddenly she was choking with laughter.

'Ten thousand pounds to get engaged to Matt! You don't know how funny that is. I'd say "yes" to him to-morrow—without any payment.'

Tom looked astounded. 'You would?'

'I'm in love with him, you idiot, and my one hope is that he *will* propose to me.'

'You really mean that? I thought you were stringing him along in the hope that he'd throw more work our way.'

'Well, you were wrong,' she assured him.

'I'm sure Mark doesn't think you're in love with him,' said Tom.

'Why not?'

'Because he's not in our class.'

'He certainly isn't!' For the first time Caroline felt dislike for her brother. 'He's streets above you and Mark. If he was asked a favour by a friend he'd do it freely, without trying to further his own interests— nor would he be willing to sell his sister the way you were prepared to sell me.'

'I only wanted you to stay engaged to him for three months,' he protested. 'But if you love him, you'll do it anyway.'

'Luckily for you!' Her anger increased. 'You had no business borrowing money from Uncle Bill, and then gambling it away.'

'I know,' Tom agreed. 'If you knew how frantic I've been these past few weeks! That's the only reason I mentioned it to Mark. We're not *that* friendly.'

'Mark must have been delighted. He can help you, and help himself at the same time.' Caroline glared at her brother. 'I wouldn't dream of marrying Matt without telling him the truth. I wouldn't want to start our life together with a secret.'

'It would make him dislike Mark,' Tom replied, 'and Helen would think you did it to create mischief.'

It was an aspect Caroline had not considered, but doing so she concluded that Tom might be right.

'You will do it, won't you, Carrie?' he pleaded.

'You've no compunction about taking money from Mark under false pretences?'

'They aren't false. He's paying you to accept Matt's proposal, and the fact that you'd do so without payment is beside the point.'

It was a false logic, but the knowledge that the money would go to repay Uncle Bill helped to salve her conscience. She nodded, then went to the door.

'I must go,' she said flatly, eager not to see any more of him. 'I'm already late for my appointment.'

'You'll have to sign an agreement,' Tom said hurriedly. 'Mark won't hand over the money until you do. Will it be all right if I arrange a meeting with Mark at his solicitor's offices tomorrow?'

'Yes,' she said tightly, and did not trust herself to say any more.

When she saw Matt that night, he commented on her pensive mood.

'I'm thinking of France,' she replied. 'We'll be together ten days in a row.'

'And ten nights,' he added.

She did not reply. If Mark was willing to put up ten

thousand pounds in the belief that Matt would propose to her, he must be pretty sure of himself. Hope rose within her and she suddenly felt elated.

'Darling Matt,' she said, when he kissed her good-night, and was so moved by tenderness for him that she returned his kiss with unusual intensity.

'Caroline,' he said huskily. 'You drive me crazy. What can I do?'

'Drink a glass of hot milk under a cold shower before you go to bed!' she replied, and gently closed her front door on him.

CHAPTER FIVE

WHEN Caroline arrived at Mark's solicitor's Mark was already there.

'I know you don't approve of what I'm asking you to do,' he said solemnly, 'but try to see my side of it. I'll do anything to get control of my business again.'

'You mean you want me to do anything.' She made no effort to hide her contempt. 'I wouldn't be here if it weren't for my uncle, and my only concern is to see that he gets his money back.'

Mark reddened and said no more, and within half an hour Caroline had signed a document agreeing to accept Matt's proposal, and also to be bound by it for three months, or the money would have to be repaid in full.

She left with a terse goodbye and returned to her car, and once seated, took out her copy of the agreement and read it again. If Mark knew how she really felt about Matt, how furious he would be! She looked forward to the day when she could tell Matt about it. But she would have to choose the right time.

She was late arriving at the studios in St John's Wood where she was being photographed for a fashion spread in *Women's Monthly*, and the photographer was so annoyed that he peppered his conversation with crude words, knowing how much she disliked them.

By the time she was home again she was exhausted, but a warm bath revived her and she rushed to be ready by seven-thirty when Matt was coming to pick her up. They went to the theatre, and although it was a play she had wanted to see, she found it difficult to concentrate. Her mind kept harping back to that morning, and she wondered when Matt was going to propose. Mark said it would be in the South of France, but would it be at the beginning of their stay or at the end?

'Relax,' Matt whispered into her ear. 'You're as tense as a coiled spring.'

'Sorry,' she whispered back, and made an effort to concentrate on the stage.

During dinner he kept up his usual light banter, and only when he left her outside her flat did he momentarily become serious.

'Don't forget to miss me for the next few days,' he said, 'and don't fall for anyone else.'

'Miss you?' she queried. 'Where are you going?'

'I'm going to France ahead of you. Mark's lined up a big French sportswear firm who'd like to buy into the brochure, but he needs my approval before finalising it.'

'Do you think he resents having to defer to you?'

'Maybe. But that's his problem, not mine.' He drew her close. 'I'm going to miss you, Sleeping Beauty. You wouldn't like to come down ahead with me?'

'Yes, but I won't!'

'I'll be staying on my yacht,' he whispered. 'It's even more swish than your hotel.'

'But not as safe.'

He looked disgusted. 'A beautiful blonde of twenty-four who wants to be safe!'

'It's better than being sorry!'

Matt laughed and let her go. 'See you next week, then. If you change your mind you only have to phone.'

Caroline missed Matt more than she had believed possible and decided to spend the weekend with her aunt and uncle in the country. Tom had already received his cheque from Mark, and had given it to her to give to Uncle Bill.

'Tell him that my business deal fell through, and I didn't need the money after all,' Tom instructed her.

With a feeling of relief Caroline handed the cheque to her uncle, who looked disappointed that his nephew's venture had not materialised.

'If only Tom would get a job,' he said, tugging at his small moustache. 'If he doesn't settle into something soon he'll fritter away his entire life.'

'He's doing a modelling job with me,' Caroline said. 'The offer came through Mark Ingle.'

'Didn't Bishop Industries buy him out?' her uncle asked.

Caroline nodded. 'I'm surprised you know.'

'I don't see why. Bishop's doings are always in the news. He's a tough nut, I hear.'

'A charming one,' Caroline said. 'I met him some time ago.'

Her aunt pricked up her ears. 'Anything serious, darling?'

Caroline hesitated before speaking, then decided to give them a hint that her relationship with Matt might turn out to be more than a casual one.

'I don't know him well enough yet,' she added.

'But you'd like to know him better?'

'Yes, I would.'

'Don't be bowled over by his reputation,' her uncle warned.

'What a thing to say!' his wife protested. 'If Caroline was interested in money, she'd have married long ago. You know the opportunities she's had.' She smiled at her niece. 'If you like Matt Bishop go on seeing him, and trust your own judgment. Perhaps you'd like to bring him down for the weekend?'

'And get your aunt's judgment!' her uncle put in.

Caroline laughed. 'Perhaps I will when we come back from France.'

Caroline returned to London late on Sunday, counting the hours until she could see Matt. She was not sure whether he would be at the airport to meet her, and the next morning it took her some time to decide what to wear. Finally she chose a St Laurent pastel print dress, its subdued colouring enhancing the pearly gleam of her skin.

The journey to Nice took under two hours and while Tom talked to Lee Lloyd the photographer, Caroline spoke to his fiancée, Ann Webster. A slim brunette, she looked as if she would be more at home riding to hounds than lugging lighting around and loading cameras. She was an amusing girl and easy to talk to and had no illusions about Lee.

'He keeps putting off the final decision to get spliced,' she said. 'Sometimes I think he only promised to marry me in order to keep me working for him. You know Lee. It's work first, all the time with him.'

'You can always leave,' said Caroline.

'I love the guy.'

Caroline felt sorry for Ann. Lee, like most photographers she had worked with, was a bit of a lecher. Obviously he did not want to settle down yet, and who could blame him? He worked with so many beautiful girls that he would find it difficult to stay faithful.

'Have you modelled for Matt Bishop before?' Ann asked, interrupting her reverie.

'No, but I've been dating him.'

'Lucky girl! Is he as dishy as they say?'

'Dishier.'

Caroline was saved from further probing by the arrival of their lunch, and by the time they had finished Nice loomed ahead of them.

As they came out of the Customs, Caroline glanced round for Matt. To her disappointment she only saw his chauffeur, Frank.

'Mr Bishop sends his apologies,' he told her as he carried the luggage out to the gleaming white Mercedes, its black hood lowered in the warm sunshine, 'but he was called away to Milan on business and won't be back until this afternoon.'

Just the knowledge that Matt had wanted to meet her made Caroline feel happy, and she relaxed as they bowled along the highway through Cagnes-sur-Mer and then turned off the sea road into the country.

Their hotel, situated some ten minutes from Antibes, was a modern glass and concrete edifice set in extensive grounds, from which one could glimpse the sea. It was difficult to believe that only two and a half hours ago they had left a grey and cold spring day in London. Here it was like summer, and even the drabbest buildings seemed bright in the glare of the sun.

Standing at the desk while the clerk checked through their reservations, Caroline remarked on the decor.

'Mr Bishop will be happy you like it,' the clerk smiled. 'Although he has many other hotels, he always says this one is his favourite.'

She was taken aback. Matt had not mentioned that he owned the hotel. But then he very rarely spoke of his business interests. As the porter took her luggage up to her room, she reflected wistfully how little she knew about him.

Her bedroom on the third floor was tastefully furnished, with the bedcovers and curtains matching the print of the wallpaper, and the en-suite bathroom tiled in the same floral pattern. But the first thing that caught her eyes was the huge basket of red roses on a table in the centre of the room. Happily she reached out for the card. The message was short and to the point. 'Missed you! Counting the hours until tonight.' Her heartbeat quickened with excitement as she re-read the note. So was she, she thought, twirling round the room and wondering if tonight was going to be the magic one when he proposed to her.

Frank was returning at seven-thirty to take them all to the yacht for dinner, and this gave her ample time to look around before getting ready. She unpacked quickly and asked Tom to join her, and together they strolled through the hotel. The four-storey building only contained fifty bedrooms, and each floor was decorated in the style of a different country: England, Italy, France and Spain. The dining-room was surrounded by a large terrace and they crossed it and went down the steps to the garden, where wrought-iron tables and chairs were waiting to be used.

The splendid swimming pool, Olympic in size, was set amidst perfectly manicured lawns, and was flanked by changing rooms, a sauna and a snack bar. The rockery below was a profusion of colourful spring plants and led down to the tennis courts, and beyond lay lush tropical flower gardens.

They seated themselves on a cushioned hammock beside the pool, alone except for a pretty girl in a very brief bikini, lounging at the far end. A waiter appeared instantly, and they ordered soft drinks before Caroline, who was wearing a swimsuit under her dress, decided to have a swim. It did not take much encouragement to persuade Tom to join her, even though he had to trudge back up to his room to change.

He dived in from the highest board, executing a perfect somersault, which Caroline knew was not for her benefit but for the young girl.

'She's a smasher,' he remarked as he churned water next to her. 'Just what I need. All work and no play would make an exceedingly dull boy!'

'As you're in such an athletic mood,' she teased, 'I'll race you to the far end. The loser pays for the drinks.'

'Thanks for the treat!' he grinned. 'You'll have a fit when you see the prices!' With a parting splash he set off at a terrific pace for the shallow end.

They fooled around for a while, then climbed out and relaxed on the poolside mattresses, drying off in the late sun.

'Are you coming up?' Caroline asked as she finished her iced Coca-Cola and beckoned to the waiter for the bill. 'I'm going to have a rest before I change. I didn't get much sleep last night.'

'And Matt will see you don't get much tonight. Thank goodness you're in love with him—it helps salve my conscience.' Tom's eyes narrowed. 'Although

I get nightmares worrying what we'll do if you don't manage to get him to propose.'

'The one thing we won't be able to do is repay Mark,' Caroline sighed. 'I hate all this deceit. If only I could think of some other way ... Perhaps if I told Matt the truth ...'

'You mustn't—not at this stage. Wait till you've got him hooked.'

'Next time I'll let you do your own dirty work. I mean it,' she added, as she saw his slight smile. 'If I hadn't wanted to repay Uncle Bill, I'd have let you stew in your own juice.'

'There'll be no more stewing,' her brother assured her. 'I'm a reformed character.'

With a grunt Caroline stood up. 'Coming?'

'I'll stay down a little longer,' said Tom, throwing a quick glance at the girl at the far end of the pool.

'I'm so glad you've found something to take *your* mind off *my* pressing problem!' she commented dryly, and walked off to her room.

After a shower she lay down to rest, but was far too tense to relax, and she wandered round the room.

Of course Tom was right. She dared not tell Matt the truth yet. His trust in her was far too delicately balanced, and it would not take much to tip the scales back again and convince him she was only interested in him for his money. She sometimes wondered if she would ever be able to tell him the truth. But once again she put that unpleasant thought aside. The thing to do was to get over this first hurdle. Once past the winning post it should be easy to convince him he had picked himself a winner in the love stakes. Or would it? With his strong feeling for honesty would he forgive her for her initial deception? That was the crux of the matter.

When the time came for her to dress, she changed three times, flinging each garment on the floor without care, in her anxiety to find something suitable.

Finally she chose one of her most simple dresses, a deep blue chiffon whose bare top enhanced the fine bones of her shoulders and turned her fair hair to silver. Excitement added colour to her high cheekbones, and she knew that Matt would not see her as a sleeping beauty tonight, but as a girl on the brink of awakening.

When Tom called for her he was formally attired in a white dinner jacket. He grinned at her expression as he came into her room.

'Aren't you rather overdressed?' she asked.

'I'm not planning to go with you. I've got a date with that smasher who was down at the pool. I'm taking her to the Casino in Cannes.'

Caroline was alarmed. 'I thought you'd given up gambling?'

'I have—with other people's money. But I got an advance from Penny.'

'If you blow that lot, don't expect me to help you out.'

'I won't.' He was unabashed. 'Give my apologies to Matt and the others. I'm sure he won't miss *me*. He'll only have eyes for you!'

'What's your girl-friend doing down here on her own?' she asked, unable to contain her curiosity.

'Chantal's her name, and she's not on her own—or at least only during the week. Her husband joins her from Paris at the weekends. She's been terribly bored, poor dear. Until we arrived, she was the only one here under sixty!'

'That's probably the reason her husband thought it safe to leave her here,' Caroline retorted. 'Don't forget we have to be up early.'

'A short, well-deserved sleep is better than a long restless one!'

Against her will she laughed, then made her way down to the lobby, where Lee and Ann were waiting by the Mercedes. Their descent to the coast was swift and they were soon driving through the ancient stone arch that led to Antibes harbour. Hundreds of boats were moored there, although most were not in use, as it was too early in the year. The variety of craft was endless—sailing boats, cabin cruisers and motorboats —but Matt's yacht, *Mystique*, dwarfed them all, its blue and white painted hull giving it the appearance of a mini-liner.

Matt stood at the top of the gangway, tanned and handsome and casually dressed in navy slacks and open-necked sports shirt, that disclosed the dark hairs on his chest. His wide, sensual mouth broke into a friendly smile as he welcomed Lee and Ann, though the smile lightened as he turned his attention to Caroline, his eyes devouring her hungrily.

'You look wonderful,' he said as he kissed her. 'I've missed you,' he whispered, his heartbeat quickening to match her own as he felt her response.

'I've missed you too,' she admitted. 'Thank you for the flowers. They were lovely.'

'Red roses for a blue lady!' he grinned, and walked with her across the deck where Mark and Helen were waiting.

'Welcome aboard,' said Helen, sounding as if she were welcoming Caroline to a funeral. No doubt if Helen had had her way, the dinner party would have been turned into a wake!

Over cocktails in the main saloon they all chatted amiably, though Helen tried to address as few remarks as possible to Caroline.

'Your hotel is lovely,' Caroline turned to Matt. 'Why didn't you tell me it was yours?'

'I thought you knew.' His eyes caressed her. 'I only send my special friends there.'

'Business friends or girl-friends?' she teased.

'Both,' he replied, then added with a glint in his eyes: 'If you want, you can stay here. This is one place where I can guarantee the room service!'

Dinner was announced before she could reply and Matt propelled her towards the main deck, seating her next to him. The night was exceptionally mild and because of it they ate under the orange and white fringed awning. The boats around them were in darkness, but the harbour lights glowed softly, reflecting on the water and turning it to black satin.

Caroline felt as if she was in fairyland. Candles flickered in Baccarat crystal holders on the glass-topped table, and orchids lay scattered between the plates. A sigh escaped her and Matt was quick to hear it.

'Tired?' he asked.

'No,' she smiled. 'Happy.'

'So am I.'

Before he could elaborate, Helen called to him from the other side of the table, and he obediently turned his attention towards her. Some of Caroline's happiness ebbed. Helen might be engaged to Mark, but she was still determined to retain her hold upon Matt.

The dinner was half way through before he was again able to talk to Caroline, and because she was irritated with him—did he always have to do as Helen ordered?—she refused to let him return to anything intimate.

'You have a superb cook,' she said brightly.

'I know. He used to work in one of the best restaurants in Cannes.'

'How did you persuade him to leave?'

'By offering him more money. That never fails—with anyone.'

Caroline trembled and was glad he could not read her thoughts.

'Do you spend enough time here to warrant a full-time chef?' she asked.

'I come here often—but only for days at a time, and it's impossible to get decent help on a temporary basis. This way, if I feel like coming down on the spur of the moment, I know I don't have to worry.'

She did not reply. How little one worried about money when one had a surfeit of it. She tried to imagine the cost of running a boat this size and boggled at the sum.

'What next?' asked Matt, and with a start she saw a waiter standing beside her with a small sweet trolley.

'I should only have fruit,' she replied.

'But you won't?'

'I never do what I should.'

'Only where food is concerned!' he grunted. 'Whatever I offer, you always refuse.'

'Then you should make me an offer I can't refuse.'

'I might at that.' He did not elaborate. 'Let's have coffee inside.'

They moved into the elegantly pine-panelled saloon, and Caroline strolled over to look at the Bonnard still life. Although she knew Matt regarded the yacht as another home, she could not believe he would keep such a valuable painting here.

'They're exquisite,' she said as Matt joined her when she moved on to a small Renoir portrait of a young girl. 'But surely this can't be a very safe place to keep them?'

'Safer than you imagine. The yacht is alarmed and there's always someone on board. In any case, there's no point having beautiful possessions if you're going to keep them locked away in a vault.'

'I like the pictures you have in your home too,' she told him.

'At one time I collected purely as a hedge against inflation. I very often didn't even bother to inspect what my agent had bought.'

'Another William Randolph Hearst?' she asked with a smile.

'Hardly,' he replied dryly. 'My humble collection would fit into one of the maids' bedrooms at San Simeon!'

'What happened to arouse your interest, then?' she asked.

'I went to a Sotheby's auction one morning. I'd never been before and it was an eye-opener to me. The challenge of outbidding a rival is something that appeals to my competitive nature—although there's always the danger of being carried away. I occasionally was at first—but I soon learned. Since then I've attended sales all over the world and learned to appreciate what I buy.'

'Don't you think it's time Caroline went home?' Helen called from across the room. 'Lee wants to start work early in the morning.'

Knowing how quick a camera lens was at picking up fatigue, Caroline conceded that Helen had a point, though Matt did not appear to appreciate it.

'I'll drive you back to the hotel,' he told her. 'Lee and Ann can take the other car.'

Wondering if this was the moment she had been anxiously awaiting, Caroline said goodnight to Mark and Helen, and carefully made her way down the gangplank.

'The sooner Helen marries Mark, the better,' said Matt as they drove out of the harbour. 'I think she's jealous of your past relationship with him.'

'Or my relationship with you?'

'I can't think why she should be. If I were off her hands it would stop her worrying about me. She watches over me like a mother hen.'

'Or a jealous woman.'

'Don't be silly.' He dismissed the idea and took her hand in his. 'Let's not talk about Helen. Right now all I want is to talk about us.'

With a sudden squeal of brakes he brought the car to a halt at the side of the deserted country road and pulled her into his arms.

Caroline surrendered to his embrace, knowing this was what she had been longing for since they had been apart. Her senses became alive at his touch and she drowned in the ecstasy of their kiss. Her desire mounted and she pressed closer to him.

'Matt darling,' she murmured, her body trembling. The sound of her own voice reawakened her sensibilities and she forced herself to draw away, knowing she would be lost unless she did.

'Don't move,' Matt held her tightly. 'I've never wanted a woman as much as I want you. Each time I see you, I want you more.'

She did not trust herself to speak, but instead brushed back her hair which had tumbled over her face.

He stopped her with his hand. 'You look even more desirable when you're untidy. It's how I picture you when we're apart—wanton and abandoned.'

'But not in your car,' she joked shakily.

'No,' he said. 'In my bed!' and with a quick flick of a switch, the front seats tilted back.

Caroline struggled to sit up, so furious she was speechless. But Matt held her down, and only as he bent lower over her did she realise his body was shaking with laughter.

'If you could have seen the expression on your face as you fell back,' he chuckled, his mouth against her hair. 'For a sophisticated girl, you're very naïve about men.'

'And for a sophisticated man you have a childish sense of humour!' she snapped.

'I'm sorry you didn't find my joke funny.' He pressed the switch again, and the seats rose back to their former position. 'When I do make love to you, it won't be in a car like some adolescent youth.' He switched on the ignition. 'I'll take you back to the safety of your hotel, my darling Caroline. But don't forget to lock your door in case I come prowling in the middle of the night!'

He resumed driving and she was silent for several moments as she regained her composure, and with it her sense of humour.

'It was silly of me to get so upset,' she apologised.

'And it was silly of me to play such a stupid trick on you.' Matt lifted his foot off the accelerator as they approached the drive to the hotel. 'I can't remember the last time I apologised to a woman—other than you. It's because you're so quick to admit when *you've* been wrong.' He pressed the tips of her fingers against his mouth. 'Forgive me, sweetheart.'

Gently she pressed her lips upon his, drawing back before he could respond.

'Darling Matt,' she whispered, 'sleep well and dream of me.'

'I do, every night, but one day it won't be a dream.' He paused, then climbed out of the car.

Going with him up the hotel steps, Caroline knew that tonight was not the night she had been hoping for. But she was not despondent. After all, she reminded herself again, Mark was not the sort to throw away ten thousand pounds.

CHAPTER SIX

CAROLINE breakfasted on the terrace of her room, and was halfway through her second cup of coffee when Tom strolled in.

'Good morning,' he said cheerfully, planting a light kiss on her head. 'I thought I'd join you for breakfast.'

'You look like hell,' she observed. 'When did you get to bed?'

He grinned. 'I didn't—at least, not my own. *Entente cordiale* is much more *cordiale* in France,' he helped himself to one of her croissants and spread it thickly with butter and apricot jam. 'I did more for Anglo-French relations last night than the Common Market could ever hope to achieve! And what's more, I also had a bit of luck at roulette.'

'More's the pity,' Caroline muttered. 'Are you seeing Chantal again?'

'Naturally.'

'And what about her husband, or don't you mind pistols at dawn? It beats me why you can't find yourself a single girl.'

'I daresay I could, but I doubt if she'd be as accommodating as a twenty-five-year-old with a sixty-year-old husband!' Tom helped himself to another croissant. 'But enough about my love life. How did yours go last night?'

Caroline filled him in on the evening, leaving out the details of the drive home.

'So you're still just "good friends"?' Tom sounded disappointed.

'I can hardly propose to *him*,' she replied. 'And don't expect me to give you a day-by-day account of progress. If anything happens, you'll be the first to know.'

'I should hope so! There's a lot at stake.'

'Ten thousand pounds,' she said shakily. 'If Matt knew ...'

'He'll forgive you, Carrie. You didn't take the money for yourself.'

She nodded, but was in no way reassured, and was glad when, at eight-thirty, they all piled into the Renault that Matt had lent Lee, and drove down to Antibes.

Lee was a demon at the wheel, and they tore along the narrow one-way streets, just avoiding the cars parked on either side of the road. The bustling market was piled high with mounds of freshly picked fruit and vegetables, and Caroline made up her mind to get in very early one morning and have a look around. There was nothing more tantalising than home-grown aubergines—fat and purple—and baby courgettes, no bigger than one's finger and tender enough to be eaten raw.

'Here we are,' Lee grunted, and jerked to a violent stop beside the yacht.

Relieved to have arrived in one piece, Caroline stepped from the car as Matt strolled down the gangplank, sportily clad in denims and open-necked cotton top.

'Good morning,' he said cheerfully to them, before he swept Caroline into his arms and kissed her on the mouth.

She was acutely aware of the pine after-shave lotion

on his skin and wondered if her body would always tremble when he touched her. From the corner of her eye she saw Helen staring down at them from the deck and she pulled away from him abruptly.

He followed her gaze. 'There's no need to feel embarrassed.'

'I'm not,' she lied. 'But there's a time and a place for everything.'

'Tell me the time and place and I'll be there!' he murmured, and stepped aside for her to walk up the gangplank.

He followed behind her, lightly swinging her heavy Louis Vuiton bag that contained all her make-up, hairpieces, change of shoes, scarves and accessories; an essential part of a model's life.

'I set aside a cabin for you and Ann to use,' he told her. 'You can keep all your things there and not bother taking them back to the hotel each night.'

Matt left them at the door of a beautifully appointed cabin, and Ann gave Caroline a curious look.

'What gives between you and Mr Rich?'

'I'm not sure,' Caroline smiled as if she did not care, 'except that I'm not doing any giving!'

'I'm glad to hear it. From what Lee's told me, our tycoon's got a long list of lovelies behind him, and our Helen makes sure they stay there!'

'Ann!' Lee bellowed from the deck. 'Where the hell are you?'

'Coming!' Ann called, and scuttled out.

Greatly relieved, Caroline sat down in front of the dressing table and mulled over Ann's warning as she applied her make-up. Helen was appearing an insurmountable obstacle to her happiness, and it would

be all too easy to blame the girl if Matt did not propose. Yet surely he had a mind of his own? An in-
sidious doubt began to nag at her. Did Matt encourage
Helen in her behaviour because it suited his purpose?
Was she used by him the way some 'misunderstood'
husbands used their wives; as protection against other
women?

There was a knock at the door and a middle-aged
woman came in and introduced herself as the make-up
woman.

'I do my own,' Caroline explained. 'But my brother
will need your assistance.'

As she went out, make-up box in hand, an effeminate
young man took her place. His English was poor but
he was a master at hairdressing, and could magically
change the style of Caroline's hair with a few clever
strokes of his brush. By the time she and Tom were
ready, Lee had worked out the shots he wanted.

To Caroline's relief Tom turned out to be a
'natural', knowing instinctively how to pose for the
best effects, and what position showed off his clothes
to the greatest advantage. Despite this, progress was
slow, for the many changes of clothes necessitated different backgrounds to complement them. It was also
tiring work in the hot sunshine, and they were all relieved when a break was called for lunch.

It was then that Matt joined them, helping Caroline
from the cold buffet that had been laid out in the
dining saloon.

'I've enjoyed watching you,' he said, as he sipped his
white wine. 'I never realised what hard work modelling
was. I thought you stood in a fixed pose and that the
photographer went click, click.'

'That type of shot went out with the Ark,' she laughed. 'Nowadays it's all action photographs, with high speed film and ten different kinds of lenses. It's a bit like working on a film set. The more movement there is, the more life we give to the clothes.'

'Time's up!' Lee called. 'Stop stuffing your faces. I don't want to take shots when the sun's low.'

During part of the afternoon Matt stood silently on the deck watching Caroline at work. Helen sunbathed at the far end, though at four o'clock she disappeared into the saloon with Matt, who as far as Caroline could make out, began to dictate letters to his secretary. From another cabin she could hear the noise of a ticker-tape machine, punctuated by numerous telephone calls. Even on holiday, it seemed, Matt did not relax.

By four-thirty the light had faded and Lee called a halt. Caroline went down to change into her own clothes, and when she came up on deck again Matt was waiting for her.

'I'll collect you at eight for dinner,' he said. 'There's no need to dress up.'

Promptly to time Caroline was waiting for him on the hotel steps, and she stepped into the car before he had a chance to get out, and with a swift smile at her he drove off.

He seemed in an unusually quiet mood, and even when she ventured a comment or two, she received such terse replies that she finally lapsed into silence. Something was worrying him, and she wondered if it was what she hoped. Knowing how bitterly he felt about his first marriage, she could understand his feeling of disquiet about entering into a second.

They had to park some distance from the restaurant, for there was a surprising number of cars considering it was early in the season, and they walked up the hill for a hundred yards before reaching the arched entrance that led them to the grounds of the hotel where the restaurant was housed.

Once inside, they went down stone steps into a cave-like interior. The bare stonework of the walls was softened by brightly woven tapestries depicting scenes from the Arabian Nights, and the only lighting in the room came from candles fitted into glass lamps on the tables, and into medieval-style wrought-iron fitments that hung on the walls.

'How romantic,' she murmured as they were led by the maître d'hotel to their table in the far corner of the crowded room.

Matt grunted. 'Personally I hate eating in a place where I can't see my food.' He peered at the menu he had been handed. 'Last time I was here the place was lit normally.'

'I'm quite willing to leave,' she said at once, hoping to pacify him.

'No.' He made an effort to be equable. 'It's late and you've hardly eaten all day. You must be starving.'

'I am,' she confessed. 'Do you recommend me to try anything special here?'

'There's no need. It's *all* special!'

The food, when it came, proved him right. Reluctant to force him into conversation, Caroline concentrated on her plate, and was relieved when, during their entrée, Matt had mellowed enough to apologise for his ill-humour.

'I had a frustrating couple of hours after you left,'

he confessed. 'I was on the phone to London most of the time.'

'Do you want to tell me about it?' she asked.

'I'm sure you're not interested in hearing my problems.'

'I'm interested in everything about you,' she said with honesty. 'Or do you prefer to keep your relationships on a superficial level?'

'Mostly yes, but not with you.'

She was warmed by the reply and made up her mind to say what she had been feeling for some time. 'I get the feeling you keep your true feelings tightly bottled up inside you. You're still afraid of being hurt, aren't you?'

'I've never pretended otherwise.'

'Will you go through life that way?' She was deliberately provoking him in the hope that he would put the question she longed to hear.

'Of course,' he said seriously. 'But naturally you're hoping to reform me.'

'How clever of you to guess! It's the only reason I'm still seeing you.'

He took it as a joke. 'Hasn't it occurred to you that I might not want to be reformed? After all, I can plead mitigating circumstances.'

'You mustn't allow your unhappy marriage to affect your entire life.'

Without answering Matt took a cigar out of a black crocodile case, and she saw this gesture as a termination to this particular conversation.

'Tell me what's been worrying you,' she encouraged him.

Slowly he started to speak, and as he began to sense that her interest was genuine, he elaborated on his problem, which concerned a take-over bid for a large engineering firm in the Midlands. A great deal of what he told her was hard for her to follow, but she knew that just speaking about it eased his mind, and she vowed that once they were married she would always take an interest in his business problems.

'You're a good listener,' he said finally. 'You've helped me to make up my mind what I should do.'

'Have you never thought of taking things more easily?'

'Many times, but I won't do it for the next ten years. I enjoy power too much.'

It was an honest answer, though she hoped he would not want to exercise it over her.

On the way back to the hotel, he parked his car on the beach outside Antibes. The shoreline was deserted and they took off their shoes and walked along the sand, hand in hand like two teenagers. The moon lit up the midnight blue velvet sea and frothy white ruffles of lace curled upon the sand. The air was filled with romance, and when Matt drew her into his arms, Caroline allowed herself to remain there, matching his passion with her own as he sought her lips.

That day and evening set the pattern for the next three: hard work from ten until four-thirty, and three-star restaurants to follow. Matt knew his way around the coast as well as he did London, and enjoyed taking her from one gourmet's delight to another, knowing that her appreciation of food and ambiance equalled his own.

Tom was also behaving unexpectedly well. He was never late, even though his maximum nightly sleep rarely exceeded five hours, nor did he question her again about Matt. It was Caroline herself who was getting worried. The days were going by and he still had not proposed.

On Thursday, after a particularly gruelling session, he announced that he was taking her to Monte Carlo the following day.

'We've still a lot to do,' Lee muttered.

'I'll try and make up the time,' Caroline said consolingly, as Lee drove her and Tom back to the hotel.

'Get Bishop to stop watching you all day,' Lee grunted. 'You work better when he's out of the way.'

This was a fact Caroline could not deny. She knew how much Matt enjoyed watching her and it gave her a sensual awareness as she posed.

'Damn!' Tom suddenly exclaimed. 'I've left my watch on the boat. Can we go back for it, Lee?'

'Can't it wait till tomorrow?' Lee saw Tom's face and resignedly turned the car around and headed back for the harbour.

No one was on deck and Tom dashed aboard and disappeared from sight. It was nearly ten minutes before he returned to the car, looking so pale that Caroline asked if he were ill.

'I just had a shock,' he muttered. 'I couldn't find my watch and I thought it might have dropped overboard.'

Caroline was puzzled. Tom's watch was inexpensive and she could not imagine him caring all that much if he lost it. She knew he was lying, but also knew he would tell her the truth when they were alone.

In this she was right, for once in the hotel he came to her room.

'You're in for a shock, Carrie,' he said. 'I think you'd better sit down.'

'Don't be dramatic, Tom. Just tell me what's wrong.'

He hesitated, then blurted out: 'The reason I took so long finding my watch was that when I went back to get it, I overheard Mark talking to Matt. They didn't hear me coming because of my rubber-soled shoes, and when I heard them mention your name, I listened.'

'Really, Tom,' she protested, 'must you always behave like a swine?'

'*I'm* not the swine,' he said jerkily. 'You should apply that to your hero.'

'What do you mean?'

'The ten thousand pounds that Mark gave you was Matt's. Having you sign a document that you'd agree to Matt's proposal was Matt's idea too.'

Caroline was perplexed, and seeing it, Tom became even angrier. 'Matt's a bastard,' he said furiously. 'He's going to proprose to you all right—but not marriage. He wants you to be his mistress. That's why the agreement was worded with no mention of marriage—and he got Mark to help him in the deception.'

'I don't believe you!' she gasped.

'It's true.' Tom was firm. 'I heard Mark ask Matt if he'd proposed yet, and Matt replied that he hadn't. He said he'd dropped several hints to you that he was not interested in marriage and he thought you were nearly ready to give in to him. Mark told him he should put his belief to the test, and reminded him that you weren't in a position to refuse.'

'But what about the shares that Mark wanted?' Caroline said huskily.

'There aren't any shares. The whole thing was a put-up job. *Matt* gave Mark the money and said that if he got you to sign that document he'd let him run the family business again.'

Caroline slumped into a chair. The story was so fantastic she could not believe it. Yet Tom could not have made it up. Matt knew she would never live with him unless they were married, and he had used Tom's need for money—and her own desire to help her brother—to make her commit herself to accept his proposal. But not a proposal of marriage, as she had foolishly thought. Tears poured down her face and she made no attempt to wipe them away.

Tom came over and put his arms comfortingly round her shoulders. 'I had to tell you the truth, Carrie. There's no point going on with this farce. I'll have to get ten thousand pounds and pay Mark back.'

'You can't! It would mean getting the money from Uncle Bill again. No, Tom—if Matt wants to buy me, I shall accept. Remember, I only have to stick it out for three months.'

'You can't live with a man knowing he only wants —to——' Tom stopped, fumbling to find the right words.

'To sleep with me?' she finished bluntly. 'Oh yes, I can.'

'I won't let you. As soon as we get home I'll go and see Uncle Bill. I'll borrow the money from him and then find a job and pay him back.'

'No. You'd have to admit you gambled away the first amount and that we asked Mark for a loan.'

'Maybe it's time Uncle Bill knew what a fool I am,' muttered Tom.

'I won't let you tell him,' Caroline reiterated. 'He'd be terribly upset.'

'Well, I won't let you go and live with Matt Bishop.'

'It might not be so bad for me,' she said quietly. 'After all, you've got to admire his determination to get me. He knows I'm in love with him, and he also knows how fond I am of my aunt and uncle. That's why he dreamed up this scheme when he learned you'd gone to Mark to borrow some money. He knew I'd do everything I could to help.'

'He was right,' Tom said bitterly. 'So he's won.'

'Don't be so sure.'

Her brother looked at her quizzically. 'What does that mean?'

'Perhaps Mr Bishop won't get value for his money.'

'I still don't follow.'

'It's better that you don't,' said Caroline, and stood up, kissing him and dismissing him gently.

As soon as she was alone, her self-control broke, and she flung herself on the bed and gave way to tears. She cried until there were no more tears left, then lay back on the pillow and tried to put her thoughts in some kind of order. Matt's calculating plan had been like a knife plunged into her heart, cutting deeper the more she thought about it.

Did he believe her love for him was genuine or did he think she was mainly attracted to his wealth? Either way, he still felt he had the right to use every means in his power to get her to become his mistress. It showed such cruel determination that she was closer to hating him than at any time since she had met him. Though she had known he mistrusted women, she had fooled herself into believing that her love for him would give him greater understanding. What a joke that was. Matt did not know the meaning of the word love. She doubted if his cynicism was caused by his first disastrous marriage. He had probably always been incapable of loving and had always seen women as fair game.

She wondered if she would be repulsed by his touch now that she knew the truth about him, but that evening, after they had dined in Mougins—a pretty village in the hills above Cannes—and Matt took her in his arms and kissed her, she knew that however much she despised him, she still desired him physically. The knowledge disgusted her, even though she knew it would make her task that much easier in the future.

Later, lying in bed, she tried to analyse why she should still love a man she despised. But love was not logical. For reasons best known to fate, Matt was the only man who could rouse her by his look; who made her think of bearing his children and sharing his sorrows as well as his joys. Whoever had said that love was akin to hate could well have been thinking of the way she felt towards Matthew Bishop.

CHAPTER SEVEN

CAROLINE wished she had not agreed to spend Friday in Monte Carlo with Matt, for what had promised to be a joyful day together would now be nothing but a sham. Yet she managed to keep these thoughts to herself, and waited for him on the hotel steps, looking far more casual than she felt in navy French jeans, with a narrow white plaited leather belt threaded through the waist, and a navy and white cotton shirt worn bra-less. The tight-fitting denims showed off her slim hips and long legs to advantage, and Matt showed his appreciation as he greeted her.

'Good enough to eat,' he said, and to prove his point, nibbled gently at her ear before setting the car in motion.

Caroline made herself comfortable in her seat. Her eyes were covered by enormous sunglasses to hide the signs of her sleepless night, but she felt calm and was determined to act as normally as possible.

Matt caught her staring at him. 'Admiring me?' he grinned.

She had been thinking how attractive he looked in his white safari suit, and how immaculately turned out he always was, but certainly would not give him the pleasure of saying so.

'I was wondering why the French named this the Promenade des Anglais,' she replied, saying the first thing that came into her head. It was appropriate enough since they were driving along the famous boulevard in Nice, with its rows of palm trees lining the road like soldiers standing stiffly to attention.

'Because the English were the ones who made Nice so popular before the war,' he explained. 'We also built most of the hotels.' He pointed to the twin-turreted towers of the Hotel Negresco, almost gothic in its splendour, which they were passing. 'That's one of the examples of our architecture. I find it much more appealing than these new monstrosities they've put up.'

'So do I,' she said, and then smiled.

'What's amusing you?'

'I was remembering the night I stayed there.'

He looked surprised. 'I thought you told me you'd never been down here before?'

'I'd hardly count one night at the Negresco as a visit to the South of France,' she answered. 'I arrived at eight p.m., and left early the next morning.'

'How come?'

'I came here to see a film producer—Gregory Carson. I met an American at a party. He said he was Mr Carson's talent scout, and asked if I'd be interested in doing a screen test. Naturally I said yes.'

'Naturally.'

'I checked on him first,' she said quickly. 'That green I wasn't. It all appeared to be above board, and when he said Carson was filming in Nice and I'd have to fly down to meet him, I agreed.'

'And then?' Matt asked.

'I was given a luxurious room at the Negresco and taken to His Master's Suite for an interview. I——'
She stopped as Matt suddenly pressed hard on the

brakes and pulled up at a traffic light, putting out his hand to stop her being flung forward.

'Sorry,' he apologised. 'I was so absorbed in your story, I didn't notice it had turned red.'

'Like my face when I learned what part Mr Carson had in mind for me!'

'What happened?'

'What do you think?' She half smiled. 'You can imagine his face when I turned down his offer. He was furious—not with me, but with the chap who'd brought me down. Talent scout was the right word for him!'

'So you flew home, honour intact?'

'The next day,' she said, nodding. 'But first of all Mr Carson actually apologised to me and insisted I had dinner with him.'

'So purity won the day,' Matt said dryly.

Caroline restrained the urge to hit him with her handbag and said deliberately: 'I've grown up a bit since then. I realise one can't stick too rigidly to the old-time principles. Perhaps if I was offered the same deal now ...' Purposely she did not complete the sentence and enjoyed the puzzled look that fleeted across Matt's face.

For a few moments they drove in silence, and she waited expectantly for what he was going to say. But when he spoke, it was to comment on their trip.

'I thought I'd take you via the Grande Corniche,' he said as they skirted past the port and headed up the hills beyond Nice. 'The views are spectacular.'

'You're always so thoughtful,' she said, and clasped his hand, hoping he would not notice how she almost choked on the pleasantry.

The road narrowed, then wound round and round like a helter-skelter as they passed houses precariously perched on the cliffs' edge. Only a low stone wall separated them from the hair-raising drop to the sea below, with no room to overtake if a slow driver was ahead. When they had climbed to the highest point, Matt stopped in the half moon at the side of the road and they walked over to the stone parapet and leaned against it, mesmerised by the beauty of the panorama before them.

Fabulous villas, each with its own pool, could be glimpsed nestling among the pine trees on the lush green slopes, and the cliffs fell in ledges down to the coast, seventeen hundred feet below. There the blue of the sky melted into the deeper cobalt blue of the sea, glittering in the sunlight.

Afterwards they descended slowly towards Monte Carlo, precariously sited on the cliffside around a natural port that contained a vast number of luxury yachts. The town was a maze of winding streets, and buildings occupied every available site. Land was at a premium in this tax haven, and no space was too small to leave empty.

'Have you ever thought of coming to live here?' Caroline asked.

'Frequently. But in spite of its obvious attractions, I prefer to pay my taxes and live where I choose.'

'I wouldn't find it a hardship to be a Monegasque!'

'Don't be so sure. What would you find to talk about here, knowing that the weather tomorrow is going to be just as good as today!'

They drove along the Avenue Princess Grace, fronted by luxurious apartments facing the sea, and Caroline was annoyed with herself for not having brought a swimsuit. The water was clear and bright blue, with hardly a ripple to disturb the smooth surface.

'The sea looks so tempting,' she remarked wistfully.

'We'll sneak away again on Sunday afternoon if you like, and go out in a motorboat. Do you water-ski?'

'No, but I'd love to try. Do you?'

'Yes. I took it up on my first holiday here.'

'Are you good?' she asked.

'I'll let my performance speak for itself—as usual!'

He parked the car near the huge cream stone Casino and they walked up the marble steps to the entrance. Caroline had never been interested in gambling, and wondered fleetingly if Matt had brought her here to remind her of Tom's weakness, and what she had agreed to do because of it.

'Would you like to play?' he asked. 'I'll stake you, if you wish?'

'No, thanks. I've never won anything in my life.'

'Nor me. Luck is what you make it—not what the cards dictate.'

Outside in the sunlight again, she breathed the fresh air with a sense of relief, then strolled with Matt around the elegant shops adjoining the Hotel de Paris. She stopped outside Cartier's window to admire a little gold poodle brooch, with two emeralds for eyes and a cap of rubies on his head.

'I love poodles,' she exclaimed, and tried to look underneath the glass shelf to read the price tag.

'Why don't you stand on your head?' Matt laughed, and drew her away to look at a boutique selling exquisite hand-painted scarves.

She was so absorbed looking at them and debating

whether to buy one that she did not realise Matt was no longer with her until, turning to say something to him, she spied him coming out of Cartier's. He strode over to her and handed her a small package.

She blushed and trembled, feeling like a gauche schoolgirl.

'A reminder of me,' he said.

Silently she opened it and stared at the gold poodle nestling in the black satin lining. How naïve of her not to know Matt would see her comment on the brooch as a desire for him to buy it for her. In his world, this was what his type of women did.

'Like it?' he asked.

'Yes, but——'

'No buts. That poodle's *me*. Remember our first quarrel?'

A smile lifted her mouth as she thought of the sequence of presents Matt had sent her on the day that Jane had moved out of the flat, culminating in the gold charm—a tiny kennel with a poodle peeping wistfully out of it.

'At least I'm out of the doghouse now,' he added.

And panting at the leash, she thought bitterly, but managed a misty smile.

'Put it on for me,' she breathed, and leaned close to him to let him do so, enjoying the way his fingers trembled as he fixed it to the front of her shirt.

His eyes darkened as they met and his mouth moved slightly, as if he wanted to kiss her.

'You're so beautiful,' he whispered.

'And so hungry,' Caroline continued prosaically. 'It's time for you to feed me!'

They lunched on the top floor of the Hotel de Paris,

which gave them an aerial view of the capital, then afterwards drove along the coast to Beaulieu, and walked around the bay of St Jean Cap Ferrat, admiring the magnificent villas.

'It's the first time we've been alone for a whole day,' Matt said contentedly. 'I hope you've enjoyed it as much as I have?'

'It's been wonderful.'

'It would be even more wonderful if we could be together the whole time.'

Her heart began to pound and she wondered if this was the prelude to his proposal. 'There's no reason why we shouldn't,' she answered encouragingly.

'That's what I hoped you'd say.' He did not elaborate further, much to her annoyance, and linking her hand in his, led her back to the car.

She hoped he did not intend to go on dropping hints for the rest of the evening. The quicker he said what she knew was in his mind, the better for her own peace. The game of cat and mouse must end tonight. But this time the cat would find he'd caught himself a great big rat!

They dined in the small port of Villefranche, at one of the many restaurants that lined the quayside, and were entertained by an elderly man who performed incredible acrobatic feats on a bicycle. Afterwards he came among the diners collecting money in a top hat.

'I'd hate having to earn my living that way,' Caroline commented.

'A beautiful girl like you shouldn't have to earn a living.'

She was instantly alert, though her voice remained soft. 'And who would keep me?'

'I would.'

'How tempting,' she said lightly. 'Is that meant to be a proposal or a proposition?' Tensely she waited for his answer, hoping against hope that he had a change of heart. But his blunt reply squashed all doubts.

'I'm asking you to live with me. It seems to be the only sensible solution.'

'Sensible for whom?'

'For both of us.'

He leaned across the table, his face so near that she had to resist the urge to rake her fingernails across it. But the memory of the money she had taken from Mark—Matt's money, she reminded herself—kept her hands on her lap.

'You're not the sort of girl who would give herself to a man unless she loved him,' Matt went on, 'and I'm too fond of you to want a casual affair. I know that to you love means the commitment of marriage—but I told you from the start the way I felt about it.'

'I was hoping you would change your mind,' she said, finding it all too easy to put a note of pain in her voice. In spite of having been prepared for this moment, now it had come it was an agony to hear him speak so calculatingly. 'If you're as—as fond of me as you say, how can you take advantage of my love by suggesting I become your mistress?'

'I'm not taking advantage of you, Caroline. You can make up your own mind. I'm not forcing you.'

Not much, she thought furiously. Only ten thousand pounds' worth of force.

'I never gave you any reason to hope for marriage,' he continued. 'If you misunderstood my intentions,

I'm sorry. This way, if either of us decides to opt out, we can do so without the agony of a divorce.' His voice grew deeper. 'I want you more than any other woman I've met. That's why I'm prepared to offer you more.'

'More?' she queried.

'I'm asking you to live with me in my home. That's something I've never asked any other woman to do.'

How big of him! Caroline looked down, wishing she were in control of her own destiny. If only she could refuse him, as her heart cried out to do. She hated him for his ruthlessness, for his determination to gain his objective. The game of pretence he was playing was almost more than she could bear. If only he had the guts to come out in the open and tell her he knew she had committed herself to accepting his proposal!

'I don't know what to say,' she answered finally.

'How about yes, for a change?'

She did not smile. 'I must think it over.'

Let him wait for her answer. Let him suffer and wonder if she would try to get out of that damnable contract. Fleetingly she thought of Penny, but knew that even if her friend could raise such a large amount, she could never bring herself to accept it. In the final analysis she was hooked like a fish.

'I appreciate it isn't a decision you can make lightly,' said Matt. 'But if you do say yes, I'll do everything I can to make you happy.'

'Except marry me.'

He did not reply, and on the way home he was silent too, respecting her wish to be alone with her thoughts. When they reached the hotel, he kissed her lightly on the cheek.

'I'll see you tomorrow, sweetheart. Perhaps you'll have made up your mind by then?'

'Don't hurry me, Matt.' Her voice was cool. 'When a girl's asked to accept a fate worse than death, she needs time to think it over!'

He half grimaced. 'Don't try to make me feel like a villain. I want you, and I want you with me all the time. There's nothing wrong with that.'

'Of course not,' she replied, and ran up the steps of the hotel without looking back.

CHAPTER EIGHT

THE following morning, after a surprisingly good night's sleep, Caroline breakfasted with Tom in the dining-room and she told him all that had happened.

'So you haven't accepted him yet?'

'I'll give him my answer tomorrow.'

'But you're going to move in with him?'

'That's what he wants.'

Tom pursed his lips as he studied her. 'What are you planning? I can tell you've got something cooking.'

'It's none of your business.'

Accepting the rebuff, Tom changed the subject. 'Lee didn't give me a moment to relax yesterday. This modelling lark is harder work than I expected.'

'Any work is hard to you,' she answered.

At that moment Chantal walked by, accompanied by a plump little man with a bald head. She gave them a formal smile and said *'Bonjour,'* but the husband gave Tom a shrewd, knowing look from close-set eyes.

'There goes one husband who's *not* the last one to know!' Caroline remarked to her brother, as the couple went to a table at the far end of the room.

'It was great while it lasted,' Tom grinned, and Caroline wondered with disgust if Matt would one day say the same.

When she arrived at the yacht Matt was busy with his secretary and Mark sidled over, intent on finding out what had happened between her and Matt in Monte Carlo. But she skilfully avoided a confrontation, deciding to let him ask his fellow conspirator for any information he needed.

Matt came up on deck at lunchtime, but was content to leave her alone until she had given him her answer. Caroline knew he must be feeling confident. After all, she was in debt for a large sum of money and would do anything rather than let her aunt and uncle know the truth about Tom. Just thinking of the way Matt had blackmailed her made her writhe with fury. One day she would make *him* pay. It was only this thought that enabled her to go on pretending.

That evening he asked them all to stay and have dinner on the yacht, but Caroline declined and returned to the hotel, though she did agree to spend the next day with him. She would be working in the morning only, for Lee hoped to finish all the photographs by noon.

In the event they were finished slightly earlier, and Matt was already waiting by his car, parked on the quayside.

'I've a picnic lunch packed in the boot and water-skis strapped to the boot,' he announced.

'Where are we going?' Caroline asked, sliding into the front seat.

'To a private beach further along the coast. It belongs to a friend of mine.'

They drove along the coast for nearly an hour before Matt pointed towards a large white villa set in huge grounds that led down to the sea.

'That's my friend's home,' he said, 'but he only comes down in August and September, and allows me the use of the beach whenever I want.'

He turned into the drive, skirted the house, and stopped the car less than twenty yards from the beach.

There was not a soul to be seen, for the cove was merely an inlet in the rocks, and the silence was broken only by the lapping waves on the shore. Caroline ran down to the water's edge and dipped her toes in. It felt warm and was startlingly clear, the pebbles glinting like multicoloured jewels in the sun.

'It's heavenly here!' she called to Matt.

'There's a beach hut round the other side of that boulder,' he replied, coming towards her with a black and white silk bikini in his hand. 'Perhaps you'd like to change first?'

She stared at the swimsuit. 'You think of everything!'

'Part of my charm,' he said modestly, and taking her arm he accompanied her over the sand. As they rounded the rock, she gasped in amazement. The hut that Matt had spoken of was more like a mini-bungalow. Gaily styled on the outside, it was mirror-lined within, with a marble and gold bathroom and similar changing room, equipped with a fur-lined double couch that looked so intimate that Caroline's cheeks burned. Hastily she donned her bikini. It was much briefer than the kind she usually wore, but knowing Matt, she was not surprised by his choice.

She came out into the bright sunshine to find he had already changed and had spread two large beach towels on the sand.

'That's like no beach hut I've ever seen,' she remarked. 'I expected the Madam to greet me!'

'Charles has a great sense of humour. You should see his house!'

'I'd sooner not.' She sat on the towel, aware of Matt appraising her body.

'I see it's a perfect fit,' he nodded at the two tiny strips of silk.

Caroline felt herself blushing. Being a model she was used to men undressing her with their eyes, but on a personal basis, it was quite different. 'There isn't very much of it to fit!' she laughed to hide her nervousness, and Matt laughed back and pulled her up and across the sand to the sea.

Together they swam towards the raft moored a couple of hundred yards away. Matt was a strong swimmer and he reached the raft ahead of her, watching as she clambered up to lie beside him.

'I feel as if we're the last two people left in the world,' Caroline remarked as she lay back on the warm boards. 'I've never been anywhere more peaceful. I can't even hear the noise of the planes.'

'We're off the flight path here. It's one of the reasons Charles bought the place.'

'Is he a close friend?'

'Fairly,' he replied, then added: 'He keeps this place for his mistress. His wife and children have another house further up the coast.'

'What a convenient arrangement for him!' she replied.

'It couldn't happen to us,' Matt said deliberately. 'I'd never have a wife.'

'A second mistress, perhaps?'

'You've spoilt me for anyone else,' he said thickly, and leaned over her, covering her slim body with his hard, muscular one.

Holding her close beneath him, one arm curved

firmly around her waist, he placed his lips on hers and kissed each part of her mouth tenderly. In spite of herself, she responded. Her lips parted with desire and as she tasted the salt water on his.

'Darling,' he said urgently, and undid the fastening of her bikini top, releasing her breasts from the flimsy silk. Lightly he rubbed her nipples between his strong fingers, arousing every nerve in her to a tingling ecstasy she had never believed possible.

'You're perfect,' he murmured against her throat, and gently started to roll the lower half of her bikini over her hips.

With a little cry Caroline pushed herself away from him and slithered into the water, then set out determinedly for the shore and the safety of the beach hut.

Inside the lush interior she stared at herself in the mirror, hating her trembling body and the glazed, unsatisfied passion she saw in her eyes. Her lips were swollen from Matt's kisses and she rubbed her fingers across them, reliving the sensation of his lovemaking. She pulled herself together sharply. How could she allow her body to betray her? She had wanted him in spite of everything, and again she hated herself for it.

Hurriedly she showered and tidied herself, then walked out into the sunshine, straight into Matt's open arms.

'I've been waiting for you,' he whispered against her hair. 'I'm sorry I let myself get carried away like that. But I want you so much I can't think straight.' He steered her back to the towels, then dropped beside her. 'Have you thought over my proposal, Caroline?'

'Yes,' she replied quietly, and lowered her lids. 'I love you too much to lose you, and I'm prepared to do

THE TYCOON'S LADY 111

as you want.' She heard his gasp of delight, and raised
her eyes to his. 'I haven't taken this decision lightly.
You know my feelings on marriage, but ...' Anger almost choked her, but she forced herself to go on with
this lie. 'But I also know how *you* feel about marriage,
so I ... must give in to you.'

'You'll never regret it,' he murmured, and pulled
her close, holding her tenderly at first, but then kissing
her with mounting passion. Once again at his touch
nothing else seemed to matter, though this time he
was the one to draw back from final surrender, and she
smiled at him gratefully.

'Thank you, darling,' she said softly. 'I'm not playing hard to get, but I want our relationship to begin
properly.'

'Properly?' Matt looked disconcerted. 'What's more
proper than blue sky and golden sand?'

'Our own home,' she cooed, for the first time beginning to enjoy the situation. 'Although I won't be
your wife, you did say I would share your home—
and if we waited until we were there, I'd—I'd feel
more like a—more like a bride!'

He swallowed hard, then made an effort to look
understanding. 'Very well, sweetheart. Anything you
say.' He drew further away from her. His voice was
still husky with longing, but he was obviously intent
on pandering to her romantic whim. Poor Matt, she
thought scornfully. Poor mutt, more like it! He was
soon going to discover it was a whim of iron!

Over their picnic lunch he told her he wanted her
to give up work, except for doing another catalogue
later in the year with Tom.

'If I stop working, I'll be dependent on you for

money,' she protested. 'I'd find it very embarrassing.'

'I don't see why. You'll be treated as my wife in every way. I'll give you an allowance each quarter and you can do what you like with it. All the household expenses are taken care of by my office.'

'But what will I do with myself all day?' she asked.

'Devote your time to making me happy.'

The self-satisfaction in his voice was almost more than she could bear. And once again she was overcome with a strong urge to slap his face and shout her true feelings aloud.

'I promise you won't be bored.' Matt interrupted her train of thought. 'I'd like you to run my home and act as my hostess when I entertain—which I do quite frequently. When I travel aboard, you'll come with me, of course.'

'You make it sound so exciting,' she purred, delighted she could utter the false words as if she meant them. 'I hope I can live up to your expectations.'

'I'll teach you,' he said meaningly.

She reddened. 'I meant that I'm inexperienced in running homes on your scale.'

'I'm sure Helen will help you.' He refilled their wine glasses and toasted her. 'To beautiful Caroline, who is going to share my life.'

'Share your bed,' she corrected.

'And my life. You'll be in my home and you'll meet my friends. In this day and age, that's as good as marriage.'

She smiled docilely. 'At least we can always be free of each other without any problems. I take your point on that.'

'You're never going to be free of *me*,' he said swiftly,

catching hold of her. 'You're part of me from now on, Caroline.'

Part of him, but only for as long as he wanted her, whatever he said to the contrary. If he were really sure of his feelings he would not be scared of making her his wife. Bitterness rose in her throat and she swallowed it back.

It was a relief to her when the motorboat arrived and Matt began her skiing lesson. Struggling to remain upright in the water took her mind off everything else, though after several attempts to ski, she tired of tumbling into the sea, and gave up.

Instead she settled in the boat and enjoyed Matt's expert performance. Like most competitive people, he mastered anything to which he set his mind. Backwards and forwards he skimmed across the water, skiing on one leg, jumping over the raft and zigzagging along at breakneck speed, bumping upon the waves and leaving the water angrily frothing behind him.

It was dusk when they left the beach, and dark when they drove along the narrow road that fronted the old harbour at Antibes.

'Big or little dinner?' Matt asked.

'Little, please. I couldn't manage more than a snack.'

They supped at a small café almost on the harbour's edge and afterwards strolled hand in hand for an hour before returning to the car.

'I've enjoyed this evening more than any other,' he said when he finally deposited her at the hotel. 'It's been so relaxed and easy. I feel I'm really beginning to know you.'

'You are,' lied Caroline, kissing him lightly on the lips. 'I'll see you tomorrow.'

He held on to her arm. 'It might be a good idea if we announced our engagement.'

She looked at him in astonishment. Did he mean he had had a change of heart?

'Why?' she asked, waiting breathlessly for his answer.

'For your sake. I know this set-up isn't what you'd hoped for, and it will help to alleviate any embarrassment for you, if we pretend we're engaged. After all, it's fairly usual these days for engaged couples to live together.'

Although her hopes had been dashed, she was pleased his conscience had troubled him enough to make this suggestion.

'Ours could be the longest engagement in history,' she replied dryly. 'I can see us drawing our old-age pensions and still telling our friends we have to know each other better before we make the final commitment.'

Matt looked disconcerted. 'If you'd rather not get engaged ...'

'Oh no, I think it's a splendid idea. But you mustn't tell anyone it's only a pretence.'

'By anyone, I assume you mean Helen?'

'Yes. I don't trust her, and I'm sure she'd tell her friends. Before you know it, your whole circle would be laughing at me.'

'No one will laugh at you.'

But they'll be laughing at *you*, before I'm finished with you, she vowed, and bidding him a loving goodnight, she went into the hotel.

Lying in bed, she deliberated on the events of the day. She had managed to keep her mind a blank for the latter part of it, but now, in the still of the night, she let her thoughts flow free. She had made her bed and she must lie in it. But never with Matt beside her. She had to find ways of stalling him for three months; that was the length of her commitment in the contract Mark had made her sign.

And afterwards? She buried her face in her pillow and wallowed in self-pity. Afterwards she would tell Matt exactly what she thought of him, and then put him out of her life.

CHAPTER NINE

WHEN she saw Tom in the morning, he looked even paler than she did.

'I wish you'd change your mind,' he begged. 'Let me tell Uncle Bill the truth. He'll be upset, but no more so than when he finds out you're Matt Bishop's mistress!'

'As far as the outside world is concerned, I'll be Matt's fiancée. So accept the situation and stop blabbing about telling Uncle Bill the truth. If you want to make amends, settle down and get a decent job.'

'I will.' Tom rubbed the side of his face. 'I'll take up Penny's offer. It'll give me good money while I look around for something else to do.'

Shortly after, Lee and Ann came down to join them, and Caroline announced that instead of returning to London with them, she would be going back with Matt and Helen.

'Any progress between you and Matt?' Ann asked.

'We're engaged.'

Ann gave her a friendly hug. 'I'd love to see Helen's face when she hears the news!' She glanced at Lee. 'Perhaps by the time we meet again I might also have something to tell you.'

As soon as they had driven off, Caroline settled herself by the pool. Matt would be joining her for lunch, and at noon she was startled to see Mark and Helen walking beside him too.

'Helen and I want to have a quick look around the hotel,' Matt confided. 'We won't be long.'

Alone with Mark, Caroline eyed him coldly. But he seemed unaware of it and gave her a broad smile. 'Matt's told me the news. I'm delighted for you. I'm sure you'll both be very happy.'

'So will you,' she retorted. 'You'll be getting Helen's shares now, won't you?'

'What? Oh yes, that's right.' Mark looked distinctly uneasy, but relaxed as Caroline said no more, and the silence remained until Matt and Helen rejoined them.

The girl gave Caroline a cool peck on the cheek, though the smile on her mouth was not reflected in her eyes, which glinted frostily. But Matt was in high spirits, and during lunch competed with the champagne for effervescence.

Helen kept up a shower of questions, asking when they planned to marry and many other more intimate details. In normal circumstances Caroline would have declined to reply, but seeing Matt's discomfiture—hidden to all eyes except her own perceptive ones—she deliberately went into long answers.

At last it was time for her to finalise her packing, and as she went over to the lift, Matt managed to speak to her alone.

'Why didn't you tell Helen to mind her own business?' he asked.

'I thought you'd be upset if I did.' Caroline widened her eyes at him. 'I know how fond you are of her.'

'Not so fond that I don't know when she's being objectionable.'

'She was just naturally curious about us.' Caroline was still as sweet as sugar.

'I still don't think she needed to know how many children we planned to have.'

'But children are an important aspect of marriage,' Caroline stated. 'Even though we won't be having any, I couldn't very well say so.' She made herself give a little giggle. 'It would be funny if I got pregnant, wouldn't it?'

'Very funny,' he said, not looking amused. 'I ... I suppose you'd like children?'

'Of course. But when the urge gets too much for me, I'll leave you and marry someone else. You must never be afraid that I'll try to trap you into marriage.'

'I'm not afraid,' he said soberly. 'Caroline, I ...' He shook his head as if to clear his thoughts, then clamped his mouth shut.

'Yes?' she asked.

'Nothing. Go and finish your packing or we'll miss our flight.'

This time Caroline travelled first class, sitting next to Matt, while Helen and Mark took the seats behind.

'It seems such a waste of money to pay twice the price for a little more leg room and free drinks,' she remarked as they took off.

'What's money for, if not to make life more pleasant?' Matt smiled. 'Please don't worry about the cost, sweetheart, you're not a working girl any longer.'

'Yes, I am,' she said. 'I've merely changed jobs.'

He gave her a sharp look, but made no comment, and Caroline warned herself to be more careful in her sarcasm. It was not part of her plan to let Matt know that she was aware he was behind the arrangement with Mark. She lowered her lids, and from half-closed

eyes saw him him pull out a black crocodile Gucci case
from under the seat.

'If you're going to doze,' he said, 'you won't mind
if I look through some business papers, will you?'

'Business before pleasure,' she said. 'That's one
thing mistresses must recognise.'

'Stop talking about yourself like that!'

She nodded drowsily, and then what seemed like
moments later, she awoke to feel the brakes of the
plane as they touched down.

'Had a good rest?' Matt enquired.

She nodded, and still slightly sleepy, went with him
through the Customs hall. To her surprise, Mark and
Helen announced that they would take a taxi and go
on ahead, though Caroline realised why when she and
Matt entered the main hall and reporters and photographers crowded around them. Flashbulbs and questions were fired non-stop, and Caroline clung to Matt's
arm and let him take command.

'How long have you known each other?' 'When's
the wedding?' 'Lady Caroline, how does it feel to
catch the uncatchable bachelor?' 'How about a close-
up of you kissing each other?'

Caroline wanted to run away, but Matt stayed cool
throughout the ordeal, handling their questions with
the ease of a professional. They posed for the TV
cameras, and then Matt, with a dramatic flourish, took
an enormous pear-shaped diamond from his pocket
and placed it on Caroline's finger. Flashlights popped
again, and someone asked when he had decided to
give up his bachelor status.

'When I realised Lady Caroline was not just a

beautiful body and face, but a hard-working and intelligent young woman. She and *Lord Haveling,*' he emphasised the title as if he relished it, 'are the only models for the couture side of my mail order catalogue.'

Caroline listened to him in angry silence, and sensing it, Matt indicated the interview was over.

It was only as they were driving back to London in the wine-coloured Rolls, Frank at the wheel, that Caroline furiously demanded to know when he had arranged for the Press to be told of his engagement.

'This morning,' he said. 'I told my P.R. man to fix it. This free publicity is worth thousands.'

'Do you always think in terms of money?' she demanded.

'Don't you?' he countered.

With an effort she controlled her temper. 'You could at least have told me what you were going to do.'

'I nearly did, but then I decided against it. I thought you might believe I only suggested getting engaged to you for the publicity.'

'Didn't you?'

'No!' He almost shouted the word. 'Nothing was further from my mind.'

Caroline did not believe him, and was annoyed with herself for ever having thought he had got engaged to her in order to make her feel less of a kept woman. He had done it to make himself look good. To be engaged to Lady Caroline Haveling gave him more status than merely being her boy-friend.

She glanced down at the ring. 'You can have this back now,' she said, and tugged it off her finger.

He laughed. 'It's only paste. I rushed out and bought

it this morning—I thought it would add a nice touch!'

'Of all the ...' fury fought with logic and, as logic won, she controlled her temper.

Relieved at her silence, Matt spoke. 'I've got to go up North this evening and I'll be away for two days. Is there any chance of you moving into my flat before I get back?'

'I'd prefer to do it when you're there.'

'Still shy,' he said tenderly. 'You look so sophisticated, I still find it hard to believe you're an innocent.'

'Maybe I'm putting on an act.'

'Women can pretend about many things, but they can't pretend about *that*.' He ran his lips gently along her cheek. 'It's because I'm aware of your fear that I control myself with you. But soon I won't need to, will I?'

Caroline snuggled against him to hide the smile on her face. Matt's control would have to last much longer than he realised—for ever, as far as she was concerned.

The first thing she did when she was alone in her flat was to telephone her aunt and uncle. She did not want them to learn of her engagement before she could tell them, and felt guilty at having to deceive them still further.

Naturally they were happy that things had turned out as she had hoped, and asked how soon they could meet Matt. She did not know what to reply, and left it hanging in mid-air.

Tom had arranged to take over her flat. He had been thinking of moving from his own for some time, and this was an ideal solution. It would also make things easier for Caroline, for if her aunt or uncle telephoned, Tom could easily explain her absence, and she could then return their calls from Matt's home.

She tried to contact Penny, but could get no reply, either from her office or flat, so instead she unpacked and then poured herself a large sherry, feeling she needed something stronger than tomato juice to help her relax after the afternoon's excitement!

The telephone rang frequently as friends heard the news on the radio or saw it on the TV, and she became quite adept at lying about her happiness. Perhaps she had missed her forte and should have been an actress!

The following morning, when she dashed out to purchase all the daily newspapers, the story was pretty much as Matt had predicted, the more popular dailies referring to her as the 'Tycoon's Lady'.

Matt telephoned in the afternoon to say he was driving down to London very early the next morning. He was in good spirits and delighted with the amount of coverage the engagement had received in the Press.

'When we start our main publicity campaign with you and Tom, your name and face will immediately ring a bell with the magazine readers. I've read so much about our engagement, I'm beginning to believe my own publicity!' He chuckled, but when she did not echo it he immediately changed the subject. 'I've arranged for one of our vans to pick your things up at seven-thirty tomorrow morning. Is that all right for you?'

'Why so early?'

'Because I have to be in the office at nine, and I want to be at the flat to introduce you to the staff. Then you'll have the rest of the day to settle in.' He hesitated.

'We'll only be together for a few days, I'm afraid, I have to go to the Continent for a fortnight.'

'What a shame!' She forced disappointment into her voice, while breathing a sigh of relief.

'I'd take you with me,' he went on, 'but I've a hectic schedule. I'll make it up to you when I get back.'

Not if I have anything to do with it, Caroline thought, delighted that she only had to think ahead to the next few days. Then she would have a respite before resuming battle tactics again.

How many different ways could she find of keeping him at arm's length without letting him know she was doing it deliberately? The pretence was made easier for her because Matt believed she wanted him as much as he wanted her. If only he had not tried to get her in such an unscruplous manner! As it was, he had behaved with such cunning that he deserved nothing from her.

And nothing was what he was going to get.

Promptly to time next morning the van arrived to collect her luggage. Tom—who had installed himself in the flat last night—roused himself in time to see her off. He was very subdued and did not say anything, looking as mournful as if he were seeing her off to her own funeral! As she followed the van down Avenue Road and into Regent's Park, she began to feel as if it were. It was all very well to despise Matt in her mind, but the difficult task was to despise him with her body. However hard she tried, it was impossible not to be attracted to him when they were together, and she prayed she would be able to hold her emotions in check.

Leaving her car in the parking bay outside Matt's

duplex flat, she went up the steps of the converted Nash terrace house. Even as she raised her hand to press the bell, he opened the door.

'I nearly offered to pick you up,' he said, 'but I knew you wanted to bring your car down.'

'Don't look as if I've crossed Siberia,' she said pertly.

'For you it was far worse. Please don't think I'm not aware of what it means to you.'

'I'm sure you're aware of it,' she said, and longed to tell him that she knew he had paid ten thousand pounds for the privilege. 'Where's my room?' she asked, changing the subject.

'Our room,' he corrected huskily. 'I hope you don't want to sleep alone?'

'Don't you?' she asked. 'As long as we're together when——'

'Togetherness is more than just making love,' he cut in. 'I want to hold you in my arms during the night, to wake up and see your face on the pillow beside me.'

'You'll soon be saying you want to cuddle me when I've got a cold.'

'That's exactly what I'd want to do.'

'You'd better be careful, Matt, or you'll start sounding like a loving husband,' she warned.

He looked taken aback, but quickly recovered. 'As long as I don't start thinking like one, I'm safe!'

He turned quickly and led her up to the bedroom, introducing her on the way to the butler Pedro, and his wife Consuelo, who did the cooking, as well as the Filippino maid. There was no shortage of staff here, Caroline thought, and again wondered how she was going to occupy her time.

'We're a good combination, you and I,' she said to

Matt. 'I supply the background and you supply the money.'

'I don't want you for your background.' His eyes were intent on her, and she kept her own devoid of expression.

'Am I now expected to say I don't want you for your money?'

'Say the truth, Caroline.'

'You wouldn't believe me.'

She swung into the bedroom, feeling ridiculously nervous. If she did not succeed in foiling Matt night after night, she'd find herself hoist by her own nightdress. Carefully she kept her eyes away from the double bed and concentrated on the three cases Pedro had brought up.

'All my clothes are in the dressing-room,' said Matt, pointing to the door opposite. 'So you can have all the cupboards here.'

'My clothes will never fill them.'

'Then buy more. You won't be short of money.' He saw her face flame. 'You really aren't avaricious for yourself, are you?'

'No. Whenever I've needed money,' she said deliberately, 'it's because I needed it for Tom.'

She bent over one of her cases, praying Matt would take this opportunity to tell her of his deceit. If he did, she would even remain here and try to make this relationship work.

'I've got to get to the office,' he said behind her. 'I'll see you later.'

Depression engulfed her, and with a nod she watched him go. Alone in the suite, she looked round carefully. The bed was king-sized and covered with blue velvet

that matched the drapes at the long windows over-
looking the park, and the sofa that stood alongside the
handsome mahogany dressing table was in deep oyster.
There was no television, which did not surprise her,
for she thought Matt would have better things to do
with his time in bed when he was not sleeping. But
she amended her opinion when she looked around and
saw a slim white portable in the corner.

The dressing-room was wholly masculine, and a
quick glance through the cupboards showed her rows
of suits and drawer upon drawer of shirts, sweaters and
underwear. Even his shoes were treed, and she wondered whether his girl-friends were as neatly disposed
of as his clothes. Where would she be hung away when
she was no longer needed?

She looked around for photographs, but only found
one of Matt's parents, faded and sad, and looking the
more so by virtue of the smart silver frame surround-
ing them. Hastily she turned away from it, not wishing to see Matt as a loving son. For as long as he did
not tell her the truth about the way he had forced her
to accept him, she wanted to think of him only as
a ruthless man.

She wandered downstairs and through the other
rooms. They all bore a decorator's stamp, and though
she admired the antiques and Persian and Chinese
carpets, she only felt at home in the sitting-room, which
was much more of a hodge-podge.

She browsed through the books. There was everything from the latest best-seller to thrillers and political
biographies, the latter being particularly well-
thumbed.

Pedro came in to ask if she wished to have lunch in the study or the dining-room, but as her appetite was at an even lower ebb than on the previous evening, she just asked for coffee.

Afterwards she went for a stroll round the garden—this belonged to Matt as his duplex was on the ground and first floor. She admired the large terrace with its white wrought iron furniture and the velvet lawns which incorporated a small pond with a cherub in the centre, and goldfish swimming below.

It was too cool to remain on the terrace, and she crossed the road and wandered into Regent's Park. Some nannies were wheeling prams, and the sight of them brought tears to her eyes. There would be no children for her and Matt, and this knowledge, more than anything else, seemed to indicate the way he regarded her.

When she finally returned to the flat there was just enough time left to change, and she chose a long hostess gown in pale turquoise jersey. She did not do up the tiny round buttons on the bodice, and as she moved the curves of her breasts were provocatively visible.

Matt knocked on the door and came in as she was about to go downstairs. 'You look stunning,' he said. 'Settled in?'

'I feel quite at home,' she lied.

'Good. I'll just shower and change. Stay with me?' Seeing her colour, he chuckled. 'I always thought models were used to seeing people in different states of undress.'

'Only other women,' Caroline said hastily.

She fled before he could make any further comment, and was sipping a glass of champagne when he came into the study.

'I love the flat,' she said, racking her brains for something suitable to say. 'Particularly this room.'

Matt's face glowed with pleasure. 'This is the only one I had a hand in furnishing. I left the rest to Helen and an interior decorator. If you want to change the other rooms, go ahead. I told you I want you to feel at home here.'

'There *are* a few alterations I'd like to make.' She decided to alter everything. That would put Helen's nose out of joint. 'It would be one way of occupying my time.'

'Still worried you'll miss work?' Matt chided. 'I thought it was every woman's ambition to lead a life of leisure.'

'Total leisure would bore me.'

'So what would you like to do? I can give you money to start a business.'

The thought of taking more money from him almost made her choke on her champagne.

'I'm not clever enough for that,' she said.

'Of course you are. Think it over, darling. If you need any cash, let me know. We may have some problems between us, but money won't be one of them.'

At dinner, Caroline could barely do justice to Consuelo's cooking—which was excellent—though she drank several glasses of champagne.

'You've drunk nearly half a bottle,' Matt remonstrated as she tried to stifle a hiccup over her black coffee, 'but you've hardly eaten a thing.'

'I'm nervous,' she replied coyly, and took his hand.

With an effort she kissed each finger lingeringly. The ormolu clock on the mantelpiece struck ten, and Matt checked his watch.

'Shall we go up now?' he asked.

Longing to kick him, Caroline smiled tenderly and nodded, and with his arm encircling her waist, they mounted the staircase.

The bedroom was only lit by the lamps on either side of the bed, and the cover had been turned down to reveal blue silk sheets. On a small glass table stood a bottle of champagne in a silver bucket. Caroline had asked Pedro to place one in the room, but he had informed her that Mr Bishop had already made the same request.

'I'll get undressed and have a quick bath,' Caroline said.

Matt looked dismayed. 'You only had one a couple of hours ago!'

Her gaze was reproachful enough to make him feel like a plebeian hog, and biting back a desire to laugh in his face, she left the room.

Alone in the bathroom, she immediately swallowed two sleeping pills, then sat on the edge of the bath and let the water pour into it and out of it again, while she just dipped in her toes. But inevitably she had to put on her nightgown, a gossamer affair of satin and lace, that left little to the imagination. She eyed herself in the long mirror, then liberally splashed herself with Madame Rochas. This should make Matt's temperature rise. She only hoped she had the strength of mind to douse it before it went sky-high!

Perspiration dampened her brow, and she pushed her hair away from her face. It shone like palest gold and tumbled freely over her shoulders. Totally without conceit, she knew she had never looked more beautiful and desirable. Her slight tan enhanced the pure white of her nightgown, and the champagne had heightened the colour in her cheeks, giving them a rosy glow.

Matt was opening the champagne when she entered the room. He wore cream silk pyjamas and a Sulka dressing gown, in black and cream. He looked so vital that she longed to rush straight into his arms, but instead she glided towards him, swaying provocatively, and ensuring that every part of her body was outlined as she moved.

Matt stared at her, transfixed, and she heard the catch of his breath. His eyes glazed with desire, but he said nothing—as if not wanting to break the spell she had cast over him. Silently he handed her a glass of champagne, and without waiting for him to pour his own, she gulped it down.

Plan one was beginning.

Skirting the bed, she seated herself on the velvet day-bed and held out her empty glass.

'More, please.'

'There's no need to be nervous, darling,' he said.

'I'm not drinking because I'm nervous,' she smiled. 'Just thirsty.'

She rattled the glass at him again, and reluctantly he filled it. Once more she drank it at a gulp, and hoped desperately she was not going to make herself sick.

'These are very small glasses,' she hiccuped, 'or else you're very mean with the champagne.'

Put on his mettle, Matt replenished her glass, then

came to sit beside her. He was trembling, and as she saw it, Caroline's heart began to pound. If only the sleeping pills would begin to work!

'Don't you think you've had enough to drink?' Matt asked huskily.

'Don't be impatient, darling. Good things are always worth waiting for.'

He smiled and leaned behind her to press a button on the wall. Immediately the velvet tones of Frank Sinatra singing 'The Nearness of You' wafted faintly through a speaker hidden behind the curtains.

Matt pulled her up and slowly they swayed in time to the music, barely moving, only clinging together, their arms entwined around each other. Caroline pressed her hands on the back of his head and ran her fingers through the thick hair. Her heart was racing and her breasts swelled with desire as she felt the weight of his body brushing lightly to and fro against her. She was aware of his response as his body hardened, then he bent his head and kissed her on the mouth, not forcing her any further, but content to rest upon her. She trembled, and his reaction was immediate. He rubbed the tip of his tongue gently over her lips and then parted them. As always when he made love to her, her desire was overwhelming and she gave way to the emotion that flooded through her. The warmth of him seeped into her bones as he willed them to become one, and she opened her mouth willingly beneath his.

With a groan, he lifted her in his arms and walked with her towards the bed. Her blonde hair spread out like a golden plume on the pillow, and he looked down at her for a long moment, drinking in her beauty.

Unable to stop herself, she yawned. She found it hard to focus, and was even feeling too muzzy to be aware of any triumph at the way her plan was succeeding. A few more minutes, and nothing Matt could do would arouse her!

'Tired, sweetheart?' he asked tenderly, and took off his dressing-gown. He lowered himself down on to the bed and took her in his arms. As he went to slip the lace of her nightgown from her breasts, she yawned again.

'I shouldn't have had so much champagne,' she said thickly. 'The room's going round.'

'Close your eyes for a moment and you'll feel better,' he said anxiously.

'If I close my eyes I'll fall asleep,' she giggled.

'Then keep your eyes open.' He gave her a shake.

'I like your first suggestion better,' she pouted, and lowered her lids. The sound of music faded and Matt's voice came from a long way off.

'Caroline darling, keep awake!'

'Too tired,' she slurred. 'Go ... to ... sleep ...' She half raised her head, smiled at him lopsidedly, and fell back against the pillow.

CHAPTER TEN

CAROLINE lifted her lids and stared at the ceiling. Twin pistons were racing each other in her head, and jagged knives stabbed at her eyes. What a hangover she had! But it was worth every single throb.

Gingerly she raised herself. The room was empty and the dressing-room door—half ajar—showed her a rumpled bed. She gave a contented sigh. It was a relief to know that Matt hadn't shared her own bed last night, even though she had been unconscious. She giggled. How furious he must have been to have his carefully laid seduction come to nothing!

Still smiling at the thought, she staggered to the bathroom and swallowed three aspirins, then returned to have another sleep until the pills started to work.

Bright sunshine filtering through the soft curtains brought her to consciousness again and, feeling less like death, she reached for the telephone and dialled Matt's office. The switchboard had evidently been given her name, for she was put through to him straight away.

'Feeling better?' he asked.

'Matt darling, I'm so sorry,' she apologised. 'I so wanted our first night to be a memorable one.'

'It was,' he answered dryly.

'I'll make it up to you tonight,' she lied. 'I'm sorry you had to sleep in your dressing-room.'

'The experience made me feel more like a husband than a lover!' he joked. 'But don't be upset. It was my fault for allowing you to have too much to drink.'

'Nothing will spoil this evening,' she promised, and blew him a kiss down the phone before ringing off.

Forcing herself out of bed, she made her way to the kitchen. Pedro was cleaning silver in the butler's pantry and his wife was chopping onions. The smell filled Caroline with nausea, but she fought it down and smiled at them both.

'I've just spoken to Mr Bishop and he wants you and Consuelo to take the evening off. I'm going to prepare dinner for him.'

Pedro looked surprised, then broke into a torrent of Spanish as he relayed her instructions to his wife, who beamed her thanks.

'You want I prepare some things for you?' Consuelo asked haltingly.

'No, no. I want to do it all myself.'

Although she felt shaky driving, Caroline went out to do her own shopping, then busied herself preparing the coq au vin Matt had so enjoyed when he had eaten it at her flat. As she reduced down the red wine and sliced the mushrooms, she hummed to herself, and couldn't help a small smile as she liberally added a mound of chervil to which he was so allergic! Her hangover was forgotten now that she was busily preparing the sacrificial dinner! Luckily Matt did not know what was in store for him.

The young Filippino maid, Rebecca, hung around clearing up after her, and although it was slightly irritating to find utensils disappearing to be washed up before she had finished using them, the girl was so

good-natured that she did not have the heart to dis-
courage her.

In the middle of the afternoon a cellophane box
arrived from Moyses Stevens containing one tiny red
rose. Encircling the closed bud was a replica of the
ring Matt had given her at the airport.

'This is the real thing—like my love,' read the card
that came with it, and momentarily Caroline allowed
herself to believe the words. Then she faced reality
again, realising that however romantic a gesture might
appear, it was just that—a gesture, and meaningless.

The ring fitted perfectly, but for all its blue-white
perfection, she hated it. Instead of being a seal of their
love, it was a hollow mockery, serving only to em-
phasise the emptiness of their relationship.

At five-thirty, dinner prepared, she lay curled up in
the corner of the sofa in the study, a picture of femini-
nity in a blue silk ruffled dress, no sign of guile on her
face, as Matt arrived home.

'How romantic to send me one red rose,' she cooed,
reaching up to kiss him. 'After my disgraceful behaviour last night, I didn't deserve it.'

'You didn't,' he agreed, 'so think what you might get
tomorrow!'

'I am!' She raised her tomato juice to him. 'This
is to ensure I don't give a repeat performance!'

'Didn't you find anything else with the rose?' he
enquired casually.

'You mean this?' She waved her hand at him. 'I quite
forgot about it!'

'Wretch,' he teased. 'I had visions of twenty thousand quid going up the spout.'

Caroline kept her face impassive, although she was

shocked at the cost of the ring. It seemed that being
a mistress could be as profitable as being a wife—perhaps even more so!

'A gentleman never tells a lady the cost of a gift,' she
scolded.

'What gave you the idea I was a gentleman!' he
replied. 'Anyway, I hope you like it.'

'Any girl would. It's beautiful.'

'You're not any girl,' Matt replied emphatically.
'There are no strings attached to the ring. If we part
at any time ... you understand?'

'Of course,' she said eagerly. 'It's a sort of a first
instalment on my pension—for when you tire of me!'

He looked at her, uncertain if she was joking, but
she smiled to reassure him, and he smiled back and
looked relieved.

'I wasn't sure if you'd accept it, but I wanted to
show you how I felt about you, and the regard I have
for you.' He stumbled over his words. 'Oh, hell! You
know what I'm trying to say. But I find it difficult to
express myself with you. You make me feel like a
tongue-tied schoolboy. I'm not usually at a loss for
words.'

It's because of your guilty conscience, she thought,
but did not voice it aloud. What *was* he trying to tell
her? Or didn't he know himself how he felt?

'What are you wearing that for?' he asked, pointing
to the frilled apron around her waist.

'I'm being very domesticated and cooking the
dinner,' she said demurely. 'I've given the staff the
evening off and I'm going to serve you all on my own.'

Matt kissed her deeply. 'Can't we put off dinner for a
while?'

'And spoil it?' she pouted prettily. 'You don't mean that.'

'No, of course not,' he said hoarsely, and ran his finger round his collar. 'What delightful concoction are you offering—apart from yourself?'

'Coq au vin as a main course. I remembered how much you enjoyed it when you had dinner at my place.'

He followed her into the kitchen, humming happily as he lifted the lid of the brown casserole dish and looked at the bubbling sauce.

'Smells delicious,' he remarked, and watched as she put the finishing touches to the avocado and prawn salad. 'You're a very good cook, young lady, this is just right,' he said admiringly as he dipped his finger into the dressing and tasted it.

'Does that mean you'll give me a good reference when I leave?'

'You aren't leaving. The hors d'oeuvre and entrée might be delicious, but until I've sampled your sweet, I'm keeping you here!'

Caroline laughed, and busied herself laying the trolley, thinking how soon he would be getting his just deserts!

They ate their meal at a small table laid in the study. The red candles flickering in the silver holders reflected tiny pinpoints of light in the Waterford crystal wine goblets, and the blue and gold edges of the Rosenthal china.

Caroline refused the white Burgundy. 'I'll stick to water. I can still feel the effects of last night's overdose.' She studied Matt as he helped himself to another portion of coq au vin from the steaming casserole. 'Enjoying it?' she asked.

'I think it's even better than last time.'

'Good.'

She removed the dishes and brought in caramel oranges with their coffee. Matt sat smoking a cigar for a while, giving her some details about his forthcoming business trip. He looked frequently at his watch, and finally suggested she went up ahead of him.

'I'll follow you up in about ten minutes,' he said tactfully, as she kissed him lingeringly on the lips.

When he entered the bedroom Caroline was already in bed, her breasts barely covered by the light silk sheet, and the shape of her body clearly outlined. The only light came from the open bathroom door, and Matt disappeared inside, reappearing a few minutes later clad in his dressing gown, the cord loosely tied. As he approached the bed, he removed it and slipped between the sheets to lie next to her.

He was naked, and his skin was warm and smooth upon her body. With a groan he pulled her close, cradling her in his arms and murmuring intimate words of endearment. He rained kisses on her mouth, then his lips travelled down her throat until they reached the hollow of her breasts. As he caressed them, she felt the swift thudding of his heart as his breathing quickened with the increasing intensity of his desire. His hands were deft as they moved over her body, awakening a response that was impossible to stifle.

'Caroline,' he whispered softly. 'You're mine now. I'll never let you go. I . . . I——'

With a sudden jerk, as if he had been given an electric shock, he pulled back from her and started to scratch himself frantically.

'What's wrong?' she whispered, strangling a desire to laugh.

'I'm not sure.' He switched on the lamp at the side of the bed.

Caroline took a moment to adjust her eyes to the light, but when she did, she gasped. Matt's entire body was a mass of red weals, and even as she looked at him the rash started to appear on his face. He dashed out of bed and headed for the bathroom.

'Ring the doctor,' he called. 'The number's in the pad by the bed.'

Richard Collins turned out to be a friend of Matt's as well as his doctor, and his plump face showed no surprise at finding Caroline waiting for him. He followed her to the bedroom, where Matt, his face puffy and red, was scratching himself and swearing.

'It's your allergy,' the doctor announced. 'How many times have I told you to check up on the food you eat?'

'I don't need to check the food in my own home. Everyone who works for me knows about it.'

'What allergy?' Caroline asked in a little voice.

'Oh God,' Matt groaned, scratching furiously. 'It's chervil. You can see what it does to me.'

'If only you'd told me!' Caroline wrung her hands. 'I used a whole bunch in the coq au vin.'

Matt swore again, then glared at the doctor. 'Don't just stand there, Richard, give me something!'

'I will.' The doctor was busy preparing an injection. 'It's an antihistamine,' he explained. 'But I'd also like you to take some sleeping pills.'

'Oh no!' Matt gave a fearful-looking grimace, which was the only smile his swollen face could give. He tried to say something more, but his lips were too puffy, and he looked mutely at Caroline.

The doctor tapped her on the shoulder. 'The injection will make him sleep, but when he wakes up, give him these.' He held out some pills. 'There's enough to see him through the night, but I'll leave a prescription for some more.' He turned back to Matt, who was already half comatose as the injection took effect.

'You look a hideous sight now, old chap, but we'll soon have you back to normal!' With these comforting words he walked downstairs with Caroline.

By the time she returned to the bedroom, Matt was asleep. His face was almost unrecognisable and he looked as if he had mumps. Guilt nagged at her and she reminded herself that he deserved it. In a few days he would be free of his rash, but she would still be tied to him for three months. Either that, or forfeit the money which Tom had already used to repay Uncle Bill. Matt's money. Her anger bubbled anew, and guilt dissolved away.

Fetching some blankets from the linen cupboard, she made a makeshift bed on the sofa. She wanted to be near Matt in case he awoke during the night, and was worried that she would not hear him from the dressing-room.

She slept fitfully and was instantly awake when she heard him stir. Her wristwatch showed seven—so he had at least slept the night through—and she pushed aside her blanket and tiptoed over to look at him.

His skin was still scarlet, and his face too swollen for him to speak distinctly. He managed to indicate by sign language that he couldn't swallow any pills,

so Caroline crushed them with a spoon and he washed
them down with water and then held out his hand to
her. Feeling like Janus, she took it and sat on the side
of the bed, where she remained until he fell asleep
again.

Only then did she dress and go down to the kitchen.
The servants were up and she told them about Matt.
He would be unable to eat solid food until the swelling inside his mouth had disappeared, so she asked
Consuelo to prepare some soup for him. At nine she
rang his office to explain the situation to his secretary,
then drove to the nearest chemist to get the pills the
doctor had prescribed. When she returned home,
Helen was already there.

'Matt looks dreadful,' the girl said accusingly. 'Are
you *sure* it's just an allergic reaction?'

'Yes.' Anxious for Matt not to awaken, Caroline
half pushed the girl out of the room. 'I understand he
had something similar a few years ago.'

Helen frowned and reluctantly followed Caroline
to the study. 'I do remember Matt telling me about it.
I was away at the time and didn't see him.' Her eyes
narrowed as she studied Caroline. 'I suppose this has
spoiled your plans for the moment?'

'What plans?'

'Don't play the innocent! I know you've moved in
with him. But you might as well move out now. He's
in no state to make love to you, and that's what you're
here for.'

Mortification made Caroline speechless. But even
had she been able to say anything, Helen would never
have given her the chance.

'If you want my advice, *Lady* Caroline, you'll get out

and stay out. You've played your cards wrong by coming to live here. Matt has a rigid code of morals where women are concerned, and he'd never marry anyone who slept around!'

'I'm glad to hear it.' Caroline found her control, and her voice with it. 'It shows he's got great perception where *I'm* concerned. You see, he's already set the date for our wedding. Perhaps you'd like to be maid of honour if you're free on the thirtieth of August?'

Helen tossed her head. 'I'll believe that fairy story when the day dawns.' She moved to the door. 'Give Matt my love when he wakes up. I'll be in to see him tomorrow, when he's feeling better.'

Alone again, Caroline was furious with herself for lying to Helen. It had been pointless. The girl would find out soon enough that Matt had no intention of getting married. But the damage was done and there was no way of taking back her words.

The ringing of the telephone was a welcome relief, as was the sound of Penny's voice.

'Sorry to intrude on the love idyll,' she said, 'but Babcock and Sloan, the advertising agency, are keen to use you and Tom. They read all the publicity about you both and they think you'd make an ideal pair to launch a new diet drink for one of the big distillers.'

'I told you I've given up work,' Caroline replied.

'I know. But this would be the biggest thing you've done. I've had John Babcock himself on the phone, and he insisted I called you and got you to change your mind. They plan to start with a series of six commercials set round the world. Money is no object and they're prepared to pay you almost anything.'

'But I promised Matt I——'

'Look, sweetie,' Penny cut in, 'being engaged is a long way from being married, and a lot can happen between bed and altar.' Her voice became persuasive. 'I'm sure Matt won't object if it's something you really want to do. But in any case it will be good for his business too if you and Tom are seen on TV. He'd be able to exploit that to his heart's content!'

They were the right words to remind Caroline of the way Matt had exploited their pretended engagement.

'How much would they pay?' she asked.

Penny named a sum that staggered Caroline. It was enough to pay back the money Mark had given Tom, and still leave enough over to finance her brother in business.

'All right, Penny, I'll do it. But I won't say anything to Matt yet. If it comes off I'll have to, but I don't want to precipitate a quarrel unnecessarily. He's going away soon for a fortnight, so try to set up a meeting then.'

The moment Penny went off the line Caroline dialled her flat and told Tom the news.

'That's terrific!' he exclaimed. 'Once we've got the money, you can tell Matt to go to hell. I'd love to see his face when you tell him you know he was behind Mark.'

'Let's get the job first,' she counselled. 'In this business, never count your chickens till they're in your own coop!'

Determined not to set her hopes too high, she put all thought of the job out of her mind, and went to look in on Matt. He was still sleeping, and she settled herself on the sofa and dozed.

Dr Collins put in an appearance later in the afternoon, and approved of the glass straw and china cup with a drinking spout which Caroline had purchased at the chemist.

'A very sensible idea,' he said, and smiled at Matt. 'You should be much better by tomorrow.'

Matt grunted and waved his hand in Caroline's direction.

'I know,' the doctor said soothingly. 'She's an excellent nurse, and you're a lucky bounder to have her holding your hand!'

'Will he really be better tomorrow?' Caroline asked the doctor as she escorted him out.

'No doubt of it,' he said cheerfully. 'But he must be more careful in future. These sort of allergies can be fatal.'

The comment did nothing to allay her conscience, and she did everything she could to make Matt's convalescence comfortable. He was drowsy from the antihistamine tablets and barely aware of her presence, but she frequently washed his face and hands with cool water, and rearranged his pillows. Unshaven, he looked haggard, and she resisted the urge to lie next to him and cradle him close. What foolish creatures women were! The moment a man looked like a pitiful boy, all their maternal instincts came to the fore and everything else was forgotten.

By the following afternoon Matt was considerably better. The first thing he did was to tell his secretary he would be going on his business trip the next evening, after which he rattled off some half dozen letters and made at least that many phone calls.

He only stopped when Helen arrived with Mark, and Caroline made an excuse and left the three of them alone. The less she saw of that couple the better. Only when she heard the front door close an hour later did she return to his room.

He had propped himself up on his pillows and he patted the bed for her to sit beside him. 'You've had a rotten two days taking care of me. I want to thank you for it.'

'It was the least I could do, when it was all my fault.'

'You mustn't blame yourself. It was my fault for not telling you.' He fondled her hand. 'It seems fate wants to keep us apart. I wish I didn't have this damned trip tomorrow.'

'Absence makes the heart grow fonder,' she answered lightly. 'And remember, your patience will be rewarded with my virtue!'

Matt smiled, then drifted off to sleep, only awaking when Pedro came in with his supper.

'Why don't you have your own meal in the dining-room?' Matt suggested to Caroline. 'You'll be more comfortable there.'

'I'd rather stay with you.'

'That's what I like to hear.'

After dinner they both watched a Western on TV, Caroline lounging on the bed, relaxed in the knowledge that the man beside her was too weak to carry out the undoubtedly sensual thoughts that went through his mind each time he looked at her. Pray heaven she could keep him this way for as long as was necessary.

CHAPTER ELEVEN

By mid-afternoon next day Matt was almost his normal self, and Caroline drove with him to the airport to see him off. 'I hope the flat will run itself without you,' she said, keeping her voice low in case Frank could hear. 'I'd find it embarrassing to give orders to the staff. After all, I'm not their mistress.'

'You're not mine either!' he said ruefully. 'But don't worry about the staff. Helen manages the household accounts and wages from the office, and if there are any other problems, she can deal with it.'

'How necessary you make me feel,' Caroline retorted.

'You are,' his grip on her arm was painful. 'If you don't know that yet, it's your fault.' His mouth hovered over hers. 'I wish you were coming with me. I don't suppose you'd like to follow me out?'

'I'd love to,' she murmured, staring innocently into his face. 'But I'll get frightfully miserable in a strange city on my own, and you said you'd be tied up the whole time.'

'So I did,' he said regretfully. 'Next time I'll keep my mouth shut. I want you with me the whole time. You've grown on me, sweetheart.'

Like a big fat corn, she thought happily, though you won't know it till I step on your toe!

'Darling Matt,' she said aloud. 'I'll count the days till you come home.'

Speeding back to London, Caroline gave thanks to the kindly fate that had sent Matt away from her. It had been hard enough to keep him at arms' length for two amorous nights, without having to contemplate doing it on a regular basis. Still, she did have other contingency plans, and would use them until such time as she could walk out on him. Or until he fell genuinely in love with her and told her the truth. Dreams, she mused, doubting if this would ever happen.

'I'm entirely at your service while Mr Bishop's away,' the chauffeur said as he deposited her at the Nash house.

'I'll call you if I need you,' she smiled. 'But I'm used to doing my own driving.'

Indeed the last thing she wanted was for Frank to know what she was doing. He might mention some of her appointments to Matt before she was ready to tell him herself.

The next fortnight passed swiftly. Caroline and Tom went to the advertising agency and met the producer who would be in charge of the diet commercials. He ran tests on them in a studio, with a draft script, and everyone seemed delighted, though Penny warned them they might not get final confirmation for a few weeks since the client had to approve the screen test too.

Matt rang her each evening and at the end of the first week she took his advice and spent a few days with her aunt and uncle. They eagerly questioned her about her marriage plans, but she fobbed them off, and though she knew they were disappointed by her vagueness, she consoled herself with the knowledge that she would not have to keep up the pretence for long.

Irrationally she missed Matt, and when Frank finally picked her up to collect him from the airport, she could not stem her excitement.

Seeing him emerge through the Customs hall, she realised how deep-rooted her love for him had become. It was a frightening knowledge, for she knew it might never culminate in happiness. However, as she threw herself into his bear-like hug, she was too overjoyed by the present to worry about the morrow.

'Hey!' he disentangled himself reluctantly. 'It was worth going away for this reception!'

Her arm linked tightly in his, they made their way to the Rolls where, alone in the back, he kissed her with burning intensity.

'Darling, don't!' she protested, conscious of Frank at the wheel.

With a sigh Matt acquiesced, but still kept her close beside him, his thigh hard against hers.

'Did you have a successful trip?' she asked. 'Each time you telephoned you only talked about *us*.'

'I like to get my priorities right.' His voice lowered. 'Which is why I'm not going into the office today.'

'I had an idea you wouldn't, and I've arranged a special lunch.'

'No chervil, I hope?'

Her face flamed guiltily, but he mistook it for contrition and hugged her again. 'Darling Caroline, I missed you desperately.'

During lunch, Matt repeated this in every possible way; with words, with touch, by the look in his eyes; and when he downed his coffee at a gulp and suggested they went upstairs, Caroline had no option but to agree.

'Give me a quarter of an hour,' she murmured, backing to the door. 'I feel so sticky and ...'

'Of course,' he said tenderly. 'I've waited so long for you, a few minutes more won't kill me—I hope!'

In the bedroom, she undressed with shaky hands. Plan three was going to be far more difficult than plans one or two and, if things went wrong, could be highly dangerous for her. But she had no option. It was a desperate measure for a desperate situation. Fleetingly she toyed with the idea of letting Matt make love to her, then instantly dismissed it. As long as she could ward him off, she would retain her pride. To become his mistress upon his own selfish terms did not bear contemplation. Drawing a deep breath, she picked up a terry towel robe and went into the bathroom.

Under a cool shower she lathered herself thoroughly, then rinsed her body and dropped the soap on to the tiled floor of the shower cabinet, and switched off the shower. Closing her eyes, she deliberately stepped on to the bar, then clutched at the side rail to stop herself from falling.

'Idiot!' she berated herself. 'You've *got* to fall!'

Once again she made the attempt, but again she instinctively flung out her hands to save herself. Shaking with nerves, she picked up the soap and stared at it as if it were a snake.

'Caroline!' Matt called from the bedroom. 'Can I come in and dry you?'

She gave a start of fear and dropped the soap. 'No!' she almost shouted the word. 'I'll be out in a minute.' Lunging for her robe, she swung it around her shoulders and stepped forward hurriedly. Her left foot came down hard on a slippery wadge and she went crashing to the ground, banging her head hard on the side of the shower.

Almost knocked out by the force of her fall, she lay where she was, barely aware of Matt rushing in.

His face blanched as he saw her and he bent over her. 'What's happened?'

Groggily she tried to move her head, but winced with pain and staggered. 'I—— I think I slipped ... the soap,' she added shakily.

'Don't move,' he warned. 'You gave yourself a nasty bang. I'll help you and then call Richard.'

Carefully he lifted her and carried her into the bedroom, where he gently settled her on the bed. She was fast returning to normal, but remembered to give a heart-rending groan as her body touched the mattress.

'My back,' she gasped. 'I think I've broken it.'

'I'm sure you haven't.' Matt's anxious expression belied his words. 'Doc'll be here soon. Lie still, darling.'

Caroline did so. Plan three was working out; all she had to do was convince the doctor. Hearing his footsteps on the stairs, she gave a pitiful groan. There was nothing like establishing the right atmosphere from the word go.

'Have you ever had any disc trouble before?' Richard Collins asked, after giving her a careful examination.

'Many years ago,' she answered. 'It was through diving, and I've been careful to avoid it ever since.'

'Well, you've got it again. The only cure is rest, as you probably know.' He looked at Matt. 'She must lie flat on her back and move as little as possible.'

'How long will it be before she's better?' Matt asked anxiously.

'Anything from a few days to a few weeks.' He faced Caroline. 'I'll leave some pethedine tablets in case the pain gets worse, but only take them if you must. Use aspirins if you can, they're safer.'

'Are you sure nothing's broken?' Matt asked.

'Positive. But it would be a good idea to get a wooden board and place it under the mattress. This one is far too soft. What a household!' Richard Collins remarked on his way to the door. 'I don't come here from one year to another, and now I might as well take up residence!'

'Oh, Matt,' Caroline cried when she was alone with him. 'What a rotten homecoming for you! And I was so sure nothing would go wrong this time.'

'They say more accidents happen in the home than anywhere else, and they must have based it on mine when they came up with the statistics!' He kissed her forehead. 'You get better quickly, darling; that's all I care about.'

He went shopping soon afterwards and returned with a large board, which he placed under the mattress. Caroline dutifully remembered to give a couple of tiny yelps of pain as she was forced to move, and then sighed heavily as she allowed herself to be resettled. The bed felt like a brick, but she was prepared to suffer for a good cause!

'Will you be okay if I leave you?' he asked after he had helped her to eat a lightly boiled egg and some toast. 'I haven't been to the office for a fortnight and——'

'Oh, do go,' she said instantly, delighted at the prospect of being alone and able to walk around unseen.

'I've arranged for a day nurse to come and look
after you,' he added. 'You might be embarrassed if I
offered to help you to the bathroom.'

Her cheeks coloured and she looked away from
him. If he truly loved her she would never be shy
with him, but knowing how he felt made a genuine
intimacy impossible.

'Do go to the office, Matt,' she reiterated. 'I'll rest
more easily if I'm not worrying about you being
bored.'

'I'm never bored when I'm with you. Even without
make-up, and unkempt as you are, you're the most
lovely thing I've seen.'

A gift that he had bought himself for ten thousand
pounds, she thought, and could not stop tears of hurt
and anger coursing down her face.

'Sweetheart, don't cry!' Instantly Matt was beside
her, cradling her close yet careful not to move her
body. 'You're feeling weepy because of the reaction.
You gave yourself a hell of a knock.'

'I know.' She swallowed the lump in her throat and
forced a smile to her lips. 'I'll be better when I feel
more rested.'

Taking the hint, Matt went off to the office, and
once she heard his car purr away, she jumped out of
bed and danced a jig. She was in mid-leap when she
heard voices coming nearer, and dived for the bedcovers, just managing to pull up the sheet as a middle-
aged nurse came in.

Sister Dickenson—'but do call me Dora'—was
plump, garrulous, but competent, and Caroline had

to keep all her wits about her to keep her fooled. It was easier to do this with Doctor Collins, for he only popped in briefly each day, but the nurse was in attendance the whole time.

'The less you move, the better,' Dora said when her charge feebly protested that she did not need a bed-pan or a bed-bath. 'I'm here to take care of you, and I don't like getting money I haven't earned!'

Slowly the days passed. Matt slept in the dressing-room at night but spent each evening with her. He could not have been kinder, and plied her with books and magazines and trifling little presents to amuse her: a toffee apple—elaborately wrapped and delivered from some restaurant that had obviously made it especially for her—such a confection being beyond Consuelo's range: a lacy bedjacket hidden inside a fur tiger: a special contraption that enabled her to project the TV screen on to the ceiling, so that she could watch it lying down.

Fresh flowers arrived for her daily, each bouquet accompanied by a note from him, to show he had chosen the flowers himself and not passed it over for his secretary to do. On the few occasions when he had to do any business entertaining at home, he always came in to see her halfway through the evening, and made sure his guests left early so that he could spend some time with her before going to bed.

All in all, he did everything and more than was expected of him, and though Caroline was furious with him for not giving her his heart, she loved him because of everything else he so generously gave.

Tom also behaved with commendable brotherly affection and popped in regularly to see how she was progressing. She did not tell him she was faking her slipped disc, having decided it was better to be discreet than sorry.

Matt always brought her mail along with him, and among the batch of letters she was delighted to find an invitation to Jane's wedding in six weeks' time. So her friend was going to marry her father's new partner after all.

Towards the middle of her second week in bed she received a call from Penny, with the good news that the diet drink assignment was theirs.

'I've told the agency you're not free in October, because that's when you'll be doing more work on Matt's catalogue, and they're arranging to start filming the first commercial in July. They really couldn't be more helpful.'

'It's nice to feel needed,' said Caroline drily.

'Hey, hey!' Penny exclaimed. 'Don't start feeling sorry for yourself just because you're spending a few weeks in bed. By the way, when will you be well enough to sign the contract? It should be in my office in a few days.'

'I'll be fine by Monday. I'll come in with Tom then.'

Caroline did not feel the elation she had expected. In a few days she would have a contract for six expensive commercials that would give her and Tom a tidy nest egg each, and enable them to return Mark the money he had given her. Perhaps that was why she felt as if the bottom were falling out of her world. Once she tore up the agreement with Mark, she could walk out on Matt. The trouble was she could not tear him out of her heart.

Tom's jubilation when he heard that they were

definitely accepted for the commercials did much to alleviate her depression, and she was almost able to look forward to their filming in Venice and then Marbella in Spain.

'As soon as we've signed the contracts,' she informed her brother, 'I'll leave Matt. I'd like to give *him* back the ten thousand pounds, but I don't want to tell him that I know he was behind Mark.'

'Why not?'

'Because if he has any principle and really loves me, he'll tell me the truth himself.'

'If he hasn't done so yet. I doubt if he will.' Tom sat down on the side of her bed, careful not to make the mattress move in case it hurt her back. 'Don't cut off your nose to spite your face, Carrie. You love Matt, and now that you've ... now you've lived with him, I don't see the point in——'

'But I haven't,' she interrupted.

'Haven't what?'

'Lived with him—the way *you* mean.'

Tom goggled at her, and with a wry smile she told him all that had happened since she had moved into Matt's home.

'Do you mean to tell me you never had any intention of going to bed with him?' he asked as she finished.

'Never. But I didn't know how I was going to do it. Like Topsy, the idea just growed.'

'How did you expect to carry on for three months?'

'By making sure my slipped disc stayed slipped!'

He looked at her with admiration. 'If Matt knew you'd planned it all, he'd go berserk.'

'He's already berserk,' she said.

Tom grinned. 'Climbing up the wall with passion,

eh?' He began to laugh, only stopping as he saw his sister's eyes fill with tears. 'Poor Carrie! You still love him?'

She nodded. 'I'm not going to tell Matt how I fooled him. He doesn't suspect a thing and I don't want him to.'

A door slammed in the downstairs hall and Caroline looked at her watch.

'Damn! I hadn't realised it was so late. That's Matt now.'

She reached for her compact, but somebody must have moved it, so she dabbed ineffectually at her shining face and told herself she didn't care if she looked a sight.

Matt strode in and beamed at her with his usual approval, before greeting Tom.

'Staying for supper?' he enquired placidly.

' 'Fraid not,' Tom said. 'I've a date.' With a hasty goodbye, he bent down to kiss his sister. 'Be seeing you,' he whispered. 'Phone me if you need me.'

As soon as Tom had gone, Matt moved across to the bed and gave her a long look.

'The only thing nice about you having a slipped disc,' he said, 'is that I always know where to find you!'

'In bed,' she laughed. 'But all alone.'

'Don't tempt me!'

'I'm sure I'll be up at the weekend,' she said comfortingly, 'and I think you can dispense with Dora after today. I managed to make it to the bathroom on my own.'

'Good,' he replied absentmindedly, and turned to wander around the room. There was a short silence and then he brought a cheque out of his pocket.

'This is for you,' he said abruptly. 'You remember that conversation we had on the beach in France, when I asked you to live with me?' She nodded, and he continued: 'I said you'd never have to ask me for money and—well, I know you don't need any for the moment, but once you're better, I'm sure you'd like to get yourself a few bits and pieces.'

A cheque fluttered down upon the coverlet and Caroline gasped when she saw the sum for which it had been made out. This would buy a whole dress shop—not merely bits and pieces.

'It's rather a lot,' she said stiffly.

'I give Helen considerably more.'

'She's your ward.'

'You're the girl I love.'

'Love?' she echoed. 'That's the first time you've used that word to me.'

'Is it?' He looked surprised. 'Well, I do. I love you very much.'

She continued to look at him, praying for him to go on talking; to confess how he had got her to come here.

'I'm starving,' he said abruptly. 'Let's eat as soon as I've changed.'

Leaning back on the pillow after he had gone, Caroline reflected miserably on what might have been. Living in close proximity with Matt these past few weeks had shown her a new side of his character. He had become a companion, not only an intended lover. But the one flaw in his character remained; his inability to give himself completely to a woman. If only he could forget his disastrous marriage! Tentatively she referred to it later that night, as he relaxed on a chair beside the bed.

'It's terribly corrosive to be bitter about something that can never be changed,' she said.

'Meaning what?' he questioned, instantly alert.

'Your marriage.'

'I'm not bitter about that any longer. The word you want is wary.'

'Wary to the point of ridiculous caution.'

'It's never ridiculous to be cautious,' he answered. 'Which reminds me, Helen's marrying Mark in a month's time.'

Caroline absorbed the news. 'Are you pleased?' she asked.

'Why shouldn't I be?'

'Knowing how you disapprove of marriage, I'm surprised you approve of theirs.'

'I approve when both parties concerned want it,' he said laconically. 'In our case, I don't, and I never will.'

And that was that. He was so emphatic, it left her no room for doubt.

Caroline stifled a sigh. She had no option but to leave. To remain with him even one day longer than necessary put her in danger. She glanced at him, her bones melting at the sight of his lean, well co-ordinated body and firm-featured face. He was not a man one could bend, and in a way she was glad of it. He had to bend of his own accord, and if he did, she prayed she would still be the girl he wanted.

On Monday morning she got up to see him off to the office, like any dutiful wife, then returned to her room and arranged to meet Tom at Penny's office mid-morning.

It took only a short time to sign the contract and

she and Tom then deposited it with her bank manager, who smiled happily when she presented him with the large advance cheque the agency had given them.

'A very handsome sum,' he commented. 'Diet drinks must sell at a high profit if they can afford this kind of payment.'

'Diet drinks and soap powder,' Tom said cheerily. 'Without them, commercial TV would collapse!'

'I'm afraid we'll be paying out most of our advance,' Caroline told the bank manager. 'We—er—borrowed some money from a friend, and want to repay it.'

'Of course. No trouble at all. This cheque will be cleared in a few days.'

Caroline wrote busily in her cheque book, tore out the narrow pink and white piece of paper and handed it to Tom.

'For Mark,' she told him. 'See he gets it at once, please.'

'A pleasure,' Tom grinned.

It was nearly lunch time when Caroline returned to Regent's Park and went up to the bedroom to pack. She glanced around the room with sadness, remembering Matt's kindness to her during her supposed confinement in bed. He had been tender and loving in a way she had not believed possible, but it was for one end—desire. He wanted her body only, but was prepared to seduce her mind, if need be, for that purpose.

As she stood among her disarranged clothes she heard footsteps on the stairs, and a moment later Matt came striding into the cluttered room, clutching an armful of brochures and leaflets. He stopped in his tracks and looked from the bed to her open cases.

'What's going on?' he asked.

'I'm packing.'

'I can see that.' His voice was calm. 'Why?'

'I'm ending our affair.'

'You can't end something that hasn't started.'

'Don't engage in semantics. You know perfectly well what I mean,' she replied coolly.

'No, I don't. Why this sudden change of heart?'

He flung down the brochures and she saw that they were travel ones.

'It looks as if you're planning to go away too,' she remarked.

'Yes.' He said no more but went on staring at her. 'I'm entitled to an explanation, Caroline. You can't just walk out on me.'

'Yes, I can.' She kept as calm as he did and was delighted by her acting ability. 'If I remember correctly, you were the one who told me that the nicest thing about our relationship was that we could part without any recriminations.'

'Now who's engaging in semantics?' he replied sarcastically, and gave her another searching glance. 'Well, I'm waiting. Are you tired of me?'

'Hardly.' She closed one case, then put her hands in her pockets to hide their trembling. 'But I've had a better offer than yours, and I've accepted it.'

'*You've what?*' he roared.

'You heard me,' she said airily. 'While you were away I had a more honourable proposition from an old friend, involving considerably more money for my services, and I've accepted.'

Matt paled. His mouth opened and closed and it was several seconds before he could speak. 'Is this old friend going to marry you?'

Caroline shrugged, determined not to lie. She had carefully phrased her words so that he could interpret them as he wished, and had hoped that the shock of her impending departure would make him realise he loved her too much to let her go. But it had acted in the opposite way. The warm, tender man she had grown to love had become an ice-cold machine.

'So you've decided to sell yourself to the highest bidder,' he grated, 'and if it includes a band of gold, so much the better. Well, it's fool's gold as far as I'm concerned!'

'There's nothing foolish about marriage.'

'From your point of view, no,' he agreed. 'It's the best way you can ensure a permanent meal ticket. Wasn't my meal rich enough for you?'

'I'm leaving you, Matt. Does that give you your answer?'

'It sure does. You never loved me. You just wanted to find yourself a rich husband.'

'Why are you so angry?' she asked. 'You can easily find yourself another girl-friend.'

'I wanted *you*. You!' he shouted, his temper growing. 'And I got you, didn't I? For all your pretended morality, I got you to live with me!'

It was on the tip of her tongue to hurl his words back into his face, but by an enormous effort of will she refrained. Matt was bitterly hurt and might possibly regret what he was saying. Because of that, she still wanted to give him the chance of telling her exactly how he had bought her.

'Yes, Matt, you got me,' she agreed. 'And you should be very pleased with yourself.'

'I'm pleased I didn't let you talk me into marriage!'

Silently she placed his ring on the bed, then took the cheque he had given her yesterday out of her handbag. Slowly she tore it into pieces, letting them fall in a small heap on to the carpet before she walked out and closed the door quietly behind her.

CHAPTER TWELVE

To Caroline, returning to her own flat—small and unpretentious though it was—was like returning to the womb. Here she was safe, could be herself; had no need to hide the love she felt for Matt.

Matt. The sound of his name was suddenly unbearable. Running into her bedroom, she flung herself on the bed and burst into tears, deep, shattering sobs that she had held in check—or so it seemed to her—from that first dreadful moment when Tom had told her of the conversation he had overheard on the yacht.

At last she wiped her eyes and shakily went into the kitchen to make herself a cup of strong black coffee.

Sipping the hot brew, feet curled under her on the settee, she resolutely tried to relax, willing herself to think of nothing. The telephone rang and she jumped, violently, almost dropping her cup in her haste to answer it. But it was not Matt with an apology.

'Carrie?' Tom's voice sounded relieved. 'I called you at Matt's to let you know I'd given Mark the cheque, and Matt told me you'd gone. I hadn't realised you were putting him to the test this afternoon or I'd have rushed back to welcome you.'

'You can do it now,' she said. 'I'll cook us a special dinner.'

'Great! I can do with some home cooking.'

With something to do, Caroline was able to pass the rest of the afternoon replenishing the larder and refrigerator—housekeeping was not Tom's forte—and then make a lamb and pineapple casserole.

By the time Tom came in, she looked more like her normal self, though she did not feel it, and trying to hide her emotional state, she recounted her last scene with Matt.

'So he didn't have the decency to tell the truth?' Tom muttered. 'I had an idea he wouldn't.'

'Did Mark ask you any questions?'

'Yes. But when he saw he wasn't going to get any answers, he stopped.' Tom looked at his sister's ravaged face. 'My advice to you is to forget about Matt Bishop. Go out with any half decent chap who asks you.'

'I wish it were as easy as that. But right now I don't care if I never see another man again. You excluded, of course!' She managed a smile. 'I think it would be a good idea if you stayed here with me for a while. I promise I'll be very discreet if you want to entertain here!'

He laughed. 'I'll stay till you're feeling better.'

Together they cleared away the supper things and, after idly watching the TV news, Caroline had a warm bath and went to bed. Another day was ending and a new one was beginning. She must forget Matt and concentrate on the future.

At ten o'clock the next morning, heavy-eyed but determined, she was in Penny's office looking for work.

'Well, well,' Penny exclaimed, 'don't tell me Matt Bishop's agreed to let you become a working girl again?'

'I don't need his agreement,' Caroline said tersely. 'We're no longer engaged.'

'Are you serious?'

'It's hardly something I'd joke about.'

Penny frowned. 'Was it another woman?'

'No. It's rather complicated, actually. I'll tell you about it one day, but I'm too upset at the moment.'

'Like that, eh? Then work's your best panacea. Are you able to start right away?'

'This minute. I know it won't be easy to fix me up quickly, but——'

'For you, anything. Leave it with me. I'll switch you with someone else, if necessary.'

True to her word, Penny telephoned her in the afternoon with a job. It was modelling a wholesale collection for foreign buyers in the showroom of a small fashion firm—something Caroline had given up doing a long time ago—but at least it would keep her occupied until Penny found her more suitable work.

At tea-time Matt's chauffeur, Frank, arrived with a package. The sight of it, small and square, told her at once what it was and with shaking fingers she undid it, desperately hoping there was a note inside. But there was nothing; only the ring. She rushed to the window and flung it open in time to see Frank opening the car door. She called his name and waved violently, relieved when he guessed correctly and re-entered the apartment block.

'Please return this to Mr Bishop,' she said. 'There's no message.'

In the ensuing weeks Caroline settled down to an orgy of work. She did not refuse any job that came her way and Penny assured her there would be no difficulty in filling in her time until July, when their diet commercials began.

Though her days were fully occupied, it was more difficult to fill in her evenings and weekends, for she couldn't face the prospect of going out with another man. Occasionally she drove down to see her aunt and uncle and also attended Jane's wedding. Her friend made a radiant bride, and Caroline found it hard to contain a pang of envy at Jane's happiness.

The bridegroom was far nicer than she had been led to believe, and though not handsome, he was ruggedly masculine, with unruly red hair and strong features.

'I'm very lucky,' Jane said with a sigh of contentment, when she and Caroline managed to be alone for a short while. 'I only hope you'll soon meet the right man.' She looked closely at her friend, elegant as always in a burnt orange Dior suit. 'You've lost weight since I last saw you. It can't be because of your broken engagement.'

'What makes you so sure?'

'Because no man in his right mind would send you away from him.'

'Then Matt must have been in his wrong mind,' Caroline said jauntily.

Jane was astounded. 'You mean he stopped loving you?'

'Oh no. In his way he loves me. But he doesn't want to be tied down.' Caroline was not sure why she was being so forthcoming; perhaps the sight of Jane as a bride had made her maudlin. 'But don't let's talk about me. This is *your* day and I don't want to make it miserable for you.'

'We'll get together when I come back from my honeymoon,' Jane said forthrightly. 'Bruce has loads of eligible friends and——'

'Don't you dare!' Caroline flung up her hands in mock terror. 'Now I've got Matt out of my system I intend to become a confirmed bachelor girl.'

Aware that Jane did not believe her, and seeing the matchmaking glint in her friend's eyes as they roamed the crowded room in search of one of her bridegroom's 'eligibles', Caroline beat an early retreat back to her aunt and uncle, with whom she was spending the weekend.

'We've booked a table for dinner at a local restaurant,' Aunt Joan said. 'We thought you'd need cheering up. Other people's weddings often have that effect!' She hesitated. 'We've also asked David Marshall to join us. He's recently become a partner of Mr Hallam, our solicitor.'

Caroline was bored by the prospect of having to talk with a country lawyer, and her aunt, recognising what she was thinking, looked reproving.

'David's a charming young man, darling. He's extremely well connected, and his father has a successful London practice.'

'From one matchmaker to another,' Caroline groaned. 'I should have stayed at the wedding!'

In the event, David turned out to be very interesting. Though not conventionally good-looking, he was attractively craggy, with heavy-browed deep blue eyes that made no secret that they found her intensely attractive.

He was a good conversationalist as well as an attentive listener, and she found that the evening passed quickly. To begin with she had to make an effort not to compare him with Matt, but by the time they left

the restaurant she was able to concentrate upon him
with all her mind.

He returned to the cottage with them for a nightcap,
after which her aunt and uncle discreetly disappeared,
leaving them on their own.

'When are you coming down here again?' David
asked.

'Not for several weeks. My brother and I are filming
some commercials in Venice and Spain.'

'Will you come out with me if I come up to Town
on Saturday?' he asked.

'I'd like that very much,' she replied, surprised that
she had agreed so unhesitatingly.

'I'll call for you at seven, then.'

Caroline gave him her address, and there was a smirk
of satisfaction on her aunt's face as she came back into
the room and saw him writing it down.

'I'm so glad you're going out with him,' she said,
after he had left.

'Don't read anything into it,' Caroline warned. 'I
need to start going out again, and he seems a safe
enough escort.'

'I'm sure he's more your type than ...' Aunt Joan
stopped and looked embarrassed. 'I'm sorry, my dear.
I didn't meet your fiancé and I've no right to criticise
him.'

'I wasn't engaged long enough for you to meet him,'
said Caroline, feeling as embarrassed as her aunt
looked. She knew she had behaved badly by not
introducing Matt to these two people whom she loved
so dearly, but the circumstances of her engagement
had made it impossible.

'You'd have liked Matt,' she said huskily. 'He was

self-made and there was no nonsense about him, but he had charm and was extremely bright.'

'Not so bright if he couldn't make *you* happy.'

'One can't blame him for that. Engagements aren't marriage, aunt of mine. They're trial balloons—and this one didn't rise very far!'

'I'm sure you'll enjoy going out with David,' came the reply. It was not the non sequitur it seemed and showed Caroline exactly where her aunt's thoughts lay.

She remembered it again when she saw David on Saturday, and found his company sufficiently enjoyable to agree to see him when she returned to London.

'I wish I could come to Venice with you,' he said. 'If you say the word——'

'No!'

He laughed. 'That was quick enough. But I'll pursue you when you're home again!'

Venice was not as glamorous as she had anticipated, but the crew and director were friendly and efficient, and they all worked well as a team. The diet drink —tasting rather like Martini—suited Caroline's palate, so that it needed little acting ability to show her enjoyment of it as she lazily sipped it, dressed in a Bill Gibb chiffon dinner dress in the bar of the hotel, or when they moved on to the terrace of the Hotel Cipriani, where they were staying.

From Venice, they flew directly to Marbella. The Marbella Club was set in extensive grounds with small bungalows, each with its own private pool, so that there were never many people around to interfere with the work of the film crew around the main pool near the hotel.

It was considerably hotter here than in Venice, and Caroline was glad to be given part of one afternoon off while Tom filmed a location shot on his own. Relaxing by the pool in the late afternoon sun, she chatted idly to Jack Morgan, an elderly American who was holidaying there with his wife. They had both watched the filming the previous day and had invited all the crew to join them for supper. He was a plump and beaming extrovert, with a thatch of thick grey hair and a quick line in repartee.

He was talking now, nineteen to the dozen, while his wife had gone to have her hair set, and Caroline was wondering how to tactfully say she wanted to have a sleep in the sun, when she glanced up and saw Matt directly in her line of vision. Her pulses gave a leap of pure joy, subsiding the instant she saw the petite redhead by his side. The girl's face was vaguely familiar and Caroline supposed her to be one of the starlets with whom he had frequently been associated before she herself had come on the scene. It seemed he was now reverting to his old ways.

'Friends of yours?' Jack Morgan queried, seeing the way her face had changed colour.

She nodded, unable to speak, and he rose lithely. 'Then I won't intrude on you any longer, little lady. I'll see you later in the bar.'

He padded off and Caroline lay back on her mattress, her pulse leaping again as she saw Matt say something to his companion and then stroll over in her direction.

'So we meet again,' he said without expression. 'You're looking well.'

'So are you.' She studied his tanned face. 'Are you staying in the hotel?'

'No. Maggie and I are on the yacht.'

As he spoke the girl's name, Caroline realised she was an actress whom she had recently seen in a TV play.

'Are *you* staying here?' Matt asked.

'Yes. We've been here nearly a week.'

'With the "old friend" who offered you such an honourable proposal?' he sneered. 'When you said old friend, I hadn't realised you meant it so literally.'

She looked at him blankly, then the penny dropped and she could barely refrain from laughing. 'Jack's very young at heart,' she replied, straight-faced.

'He doesn't look English.'

'He's American. In oil.'

'For frying?'

'Very funny,' she said, trying to look affronted.

'Not funny at all. The damn fool's old enough to be your father.'

'When two people are mentally attuned,' she said in a little girl voice, 'age doesn't matter. Don't you find that with Lolita?'

'I assume you're referring to Maggie,' he answered stiffly.

'Unless you've got someone younger with you as well.'

He glanced down at her hand and went into the attack again. 'I see you're not married yet. Is he slipping from the noose too?'

'The way you did?' she smiled, hating him for his cruelty. 'On the contrary, But he's in the process of severing an old noose.'

Matt went pale with rage. His mouth opened and shut, then without a word he stalked over to his companion. A few seconds later they left, and Caroline allowed herself a bitter smile.

She recounted the story to Tom over dinner that evening. He was highly amused, but she no longer found it funny, and was suddenly overcome by a sadness. How could Matt believe she would go off with a man of Jack Morgan's age? Did he really believe money was more important to her than love?

After her meeting with Matt, Caroline could not wait to return to England, and in the weeks that followed she saw a great deal of David. Either she went down to the country for the weekend, or he came to London. His parents lived in Kensington and he stayed with them. They welcomed Caroline warmly and made it clear that they would be delighted to welcome her into the family.

Caroline was in a quandary. She knew David was in love with her and wanted to marry her, and she sensed that the only reason he had not proposed was because he was afraid she would refuse. Yet she herself was by no means sure what she would do. She liked David very much and though there was no spark in their relationship, she was warmed by the love he had for her. If only she could stop comparing every man with Matt; no one stood up to the comparison.

She managed not to repulse David's tentative attempts to make love to her, but she could not respond the way she knew she was capable of doing, and David, who had read of her engagement to Matt, was sufficiently sensitive to know she was not yet heartwhole.

In September she spent a further ten days away, completing the final two drink commercials. This time they went to Capri and Monte Carlo. She was not pleased to be back in the South of France. It revived too many memories, particularly when she and Tom were filmed in the bar of the Hotel de Paris.

The only gift she had not returned to Matt was the poodle brooch he had bought for her. Perhaps it was because she felt that when he had given it to her it had not been for any ulterior motive but was an instinctive act of generosity—unlike the ring or the money. Oh, Matt, she thought miserably, will there ever be a time when I can think of you without pain?

She now read the gossip columns avidly, something she had never bothered to do before. Occasionally there was some reference to Matt, but he never seemed to be with the same girl for long.

She dreaded having to start work again on the catalogue, but she and Tom were contractually bound to do it, and it was with a great deal of trepidation that she went to the studio in High Holborn where all the photographic sessions were being held. One part of her hoped Matt would be there, and the other part prayed that he wouldn't. But he did not show up, nor did Helen or Mark, a fact which Lee and Ann both commented on.

'I suppose it's because Matt and I are no longer engaged,' Caroline said. 'Perhaps they felt it best to keep out of the way.'

'What went wrong between you and Matt?' Ann asked when she had a chance to speak to Caroline alone.

'He found we'd let the glamour of Antibes go to our heads. In the cool atmosphere of London, our love wasn't so hot.'

Ann looked sceptical, but before she could say anything Lee called across to them.

'Stop the gabbing, so we can get started. Caroline, put on some heavier make-up to cover the bags. You've lost weight and it doesn't suit you.'

Caroline had not realised that her loss of weight was so noticeable, but perhaps it was because Lee and Ann had not seen her for some time. Her appetite was certainly not what it had been, and she often had to force herself to eat a meal.

Throughout the day they worked hard, not even breaking for lunch, which consisted of coffee, as Lee was determined to finish all the photographs as quickly as possible. He found the project irksome and regretted having taken it on. He was the type who worked best when his enthusiasm was high, and he found it tedious to have a project carry on over a number of months—with large gaps in between.

It was seven before Lee called a halt and they were all relieved to get out of the studio and into the cool October night.

Ann linked her arm with Caroline's. 'How about coming back to our place for dinner? We've plenty for four.' She looked enquiringly at Tom.

'Thanks, Ann, but I've already got a date.'

'I haven't,' said Caroline, pleased to accept the invitation.

The knowledge that she had been working for Matt had brought back memories she had been trying to bury, and she could not face the idea of an evening watching television, as she had originally planned. That was the one trouble with going steady with David. He rarely managed to get to London during the week, and because she had no wish to date anyone else, she spent most of her weekday evenings alone. Tom was actively looking for a flat of his own again, and she was hoping he would find it difficult, for she enjoyed having him around.

Lee and Ann lived in a new luxury block off Campden Hill. The furnishings would have made Heals' glow with pride. It was not surprising, with their eye for perfection, to find such a subtle blend of colours, but they had managed to make the huge lounge dining room look comfortable and lived in —not an easy achievement in such a starkly modern home.

The blue and white Poggenpohl kitchen fitments were a dream, and while Ann prepared the steaks and jacket potatoes, Caroline mixed the salad and laid the table in the wood-panelled dining-area.

Over supper, they regaled her with stories about some of their famous clients, and she left them at midnight feeling much more cheerful than when she had arrived. Four more days of catalogue photography and all reminder of Matt would be at an end.

The following morning when she arrived at the studio she was dismayed to see Mark talking to Ann. She prayed he was not the forerunner for Matt! In her current state of mind, one sarcastic comment from him and she was likely to burst into tears. The thought of returning to him was so frequently in her mind that she was horrified by it. Only the indoctrination of her childhood helped her to stay resolute, though a moral sense of rectitude made a poor bedfellow.

'Hullo, Caroline.' Mark came up to her. It was the first time they had met since Tom had returned the ten thousand pounds to him, and she herself had left Matt, and she was curious to know if he had any sense of guilt over the part he had played in deceiving her. But his expression was guileless, and she decided that he did not care what he did, so long as it proved to be good for him. Had she not disliked Helen quite so much, she would almost have felt sorry for the girl.

'A pity you weren't at my wedding,' he said, 'but Helen didn't think you'd come.'

'I'm sorry too,' she said, smiling pleasantly. 'It would have made me very happy to see the two of you getting married. You really deserve each other.'

He had the grace to redden, and his next words showed that he knew to what she was referring. 'I suppose you're angry because I wouldn't lend Tom the money without getting you to do something for me in return?'

'That's one way of putting it.'

'You were keen on Matt,' he reminded her. 'I knew that the minute I saw you together. So where was the hardship?'

'I expected marriage,' she said flatly. 'That's why I signed the agreement with you.'

Mark looked discomfited. 'You really believed he'd ask you? You amaze me, Caroline. I thought you were sophisticated enough to know the score.'

She shrugged, afraid to continue the conversation in case she gave her feelings away.

'It's all over and done with, Mark. Let's forget it. Tom and I could repay you, and I was able to leave Matt with my honour still intact.'

Mark's lack of surprise at this part of her statement told her that Matt had already put him in the picture. She wondered why he had, for it could only have made him look a complete fool. Conscience must have made him decide to save her reputation, there was no other explanation.

'Haven't you changed yet?' Lee called out irritably, and with a nod in Mark's direction, Caroline hurried off to the dressing room.

When she emerged, Mark had gone, and with a sense of relief she took her place in front of the lights.

CHAPTER THIRTEEN

CAROLINE and Tom spent Christmas with their aunt and uncle, and David joined them on Boxing Day.

Early in January he was called away to America on business for a client, and for the entire month Caroline was left to her own devices. It gave her a breathing space and enabled her to see things with greater clarity, which made her realise she could never become his wife—or any man's wife—while the mere thought of Matt made her feel so raw inside.

Hard on this thought, she received a wedding invitation from Ann and Lee. She had only seen them twice since finishing the photographic session—once at a party, and then one evening when they had asked her out for dinner.

The wedding was only three weeks away, and the reception was at the Dorchester Hotel. No reply card was enclosed, so Caroline telephoned Ann to say she would accept.

'What suddenly made up Lee's mind for him?' Caroline asked.

'The patter of little feet. Straight after doing Bishop's catalogue, we did a big session on baby food, and one infant looked so much like Lee that the whole crew nearly collapsed with hysterics.'

'What about Lee?' Caroline laughed.

'The little brat awoke his paternal instinct.'

'Lee's?' Caroline was incredulous.

'That's right,' Ann burbled happily. 'Until now he never wanted a family of his own. No commitment, and no hassle—you know the sort of thing.'

Only too well Caroline did, and wondered if a baby that looked like Matt might turn her own world from grey to rosy.

'I'll expect to buy a layette for you in nine months' time,' she said.

Ann laughed. 'Why not bring your current boy-friend along with you?' she suggested.

'I will, if he can get away for the day.'

There was a pause. 'We haven't invited Matt,' Ann said. 'Lee was going to ask him, but I told him if he did, he'd have to have the baby himself!'

'It wouldn't worry me to see him,' Caroline lied.

'Well, he won't be there, so you can come to the wedding with an easy mind.'

Knowing she would not have to see Matt decided Caroline not to ask David to come with her to the wed-ding. But on the day itself he telephoned early in the morning to say he had an appointment in Town and was free to have lunch with her.

'I'm going to a wedding,' she confessed, and because he sounded disappointed at not being able to see her, she invited him to go with her.

It was a sunny day, but cold. Caroline could not go to the ceremony as she had an interview with the fashion buyer from a top New York store who was hold-ing an English fornight and wanted to engage her. It would mean going to the States, but she was happy at the thought. Indeed she would cheerfully have gone to Timbuctoo; gone anywhere to put as much distance between herself and the man she had so firmly proclaimed she despised.

Having been accepted by the fashion buyer, she was in a happy mood as she rushed home to change into a bottle green suede suit that deepened the green of her eyes. She noticed she had to pull the belt in a notch further, and realised she would have to be careful that her slenderness did not become skinniness.

When she reached the Dorchester, David was already waiting for her. He was easily spotted, being one of the few men not in Arab dress. His grey pinstripe suit, worn with a white shirt and Stowe old school tie, made him look exactly what he was: dependable and courtly. But dull, she thought with a pang of guilt, and knew more firmly than ever that she must break off their relationship.

'Have you been here long?' she enquired, as they waited for the lift to take them up to the Penthouse Suite.

'Only a few minutes. I ...'

The rest of his words were lost as the doors opened and she was pushed into the back of the lift by a sudden surge of people. She found herself squashed into a corner, her ribs tightly pressed by the man standing beside her, whose blue satin tie was on a level with her eyes. She tried to glance past him for a sight of David, but there was no sign of him and she inched her body back to try and put some distance between herself and the man who was still half shielding her from the rest of the people in the lift. Only as she did so did she glance up. Oh no! she thought, as she recognised the brown eyes gleaming into hers. What was Matt doing here?

She did not know whether she said his name aloud or merely thought it, but he gave her a tense smile.

'You can't escape me,' he said softly. 'I've been lying in wait for you. We've got things to talk over.'

'I'm going to a wedding.'

'I know. That's why I'm here.'

'I've come with another man,' she said coldly.

'Too bad!'

'Don't use your bullyboy tactics on me!' she whispered furiously, aware of other people listening with interest.

'If you come quietly,' he said, 'I won't need to be a bully.'

The lift stopped and he gripped her arm to make sure they went out together.

'I'm waiting here for David,' she said, wrenching free of him.

'The name's not right for you,' Matt replied. 'It would take a Goliath like me to handle a female like you!'

'Brute force *is* the only way you could get me,' she agreed, putting as much contempt as she could in the words.

'I deserve contempt, Caroline. That's why I've come to make my peace with you.'

'You could have chosen a better place—and not when I'm with another man.'

'If I'd rung you, would you have seen me?'

'No,' she lied. 'Never.'

Matt's skin lost its colour, and with it he seemed to lose some of his confidence too, a surprising happening in a man as sure of himself as Matthew Bishop.

Behind them the lift doors opened and David

emerged. 'There you are, Caroline!' he exclaimed. 'I thought I'd lost you.'

'You have,' Matt said tersely, but with feeling. 'Sorry about it, but there's no point in not being honest.'

David looked at Caroline. 'Do you want me to go?' He read the answer in her face. 'Don't look so upset,' he said gently. 'I think I always knew I wasn't the one for you.'

'Nor is he,' she said, giving Matt a look of disgust. 'I'll phone you,' she promised David.

He nodded and stepped back into the lift.

'Decent chap,' Matt commented. 'This time the best man isn't going to win!'

'Nor are you. I don't want anything to do with you, Matt.'

'Hear me out first,' he said. 'I beg you.'

'Matthew Bishop begging?' she taunted.

'On my knees if need be.'

More people came out of the lift, pushing them as they surged forward, and Caroline took advantage of the bustle to run towards the Penthouse Suite.

It was crammed full, as was the huge private terrace, which gave a magnificent view over Hyde Park.

'Caroline, how lovely to see you and ... Matt!' Ann's voice rose an octave when she saw the man behind Caroline.

'Forgive me for coming uninvited,' he said with charm, 'but I knew you'd be happy to see me.'

Ann looked from one to the other. 'I'm delighted. Help yourself to some champagne.' She stopped a passing waiter who was bearing a tray of glasses.

'If you'd let go of my arm,' Caroline muttered through gritted teeth, 'I could take a glass.'

'We'll celebrate later,' he said. 'First we must talk.'

Ann grinned. 'I'll leave you to it then.'

She went on her way and Caroline tried to pull free of Matt. 'Do you intend holding me all night?' she asked furiously.

'Nothing would make me happier.'

Not giving her any chance to pull back, he dragged her through the crowded room into the corridor.

'Where are you taking me?' she panted, having to run to keep up with him.

'Somewhere quiet where we can talk. I've booked a room here.'

Fear clutched at her stomach. Was this part of Matt's revenge for the way she had left him? Had he finally discovered how she had duped him during the weeks they had been together?

'Don't look so worried,' he said roughly. 'I'm not going to rape you!' Taking a key from his pocket, he unlocked a door and pushed her into an elegantly furnished bedroom. 'Now sit still and listen to me.'

Shaking, but trying not to let him see it, she moved as far from him as possible and sat down on a silk-upholstered armchair.

Matt was silent for a moment, studying her face and the contours of her body. 'I'm glad you look almost as bloody as I do,' was his opening remark.

She glared at him, seeing that he too had lost weight. From running around with his starlets, she thought, and felt her anger increase.

'Say what you have to, Matt, and then please let me go.'

'That's what I intend. The first part at least, but I hope not the second.' He looked at her anxiously. 'I owe you an apology, Caroline. I've behaved like a fool and I damn nearly ruined both our lives in the process. You are the only woman who has meant anything to me, and I mistrusted you, as I did everyone else. I want to apologise for that.'

'Apology accepted. Now open the door.'

'No. You still hate me—if you didn't you wouldn't look at me with such hard eyes. I don't blame you for it. In your place I'd be the same.'

'Since you understand how I feel ...' she said, rising on shaky legs.

'I won't let you go,' he said flatly. 'I'll never let you go. I want to marry you, damn it!'

'Marry me?' she echoed, and fell back into the chair.

'Yes.' His eyes softened as they moved over her face. 'I love you, Caroline. I didn't realise how much until you left me.'

'You mean you're willing to marry me in order to get me back?'

He frowned slightly, as if puzzling over his answer. 'Even if you were willing to come back without marriage, I'd still want to make you my wife.' He knelt in front of her and clasped her hands tightly in his. 'This is the traditional way, isn't it? I love you,' he said seriously, 'and I want you to marry me.'

'I'm surprised,' she said evenly. 'You haven't acted as if you missed me.'

'Because I was trying to get you out of my mind. But I couldn't. I went from one bed to another, but it was all meaningless. Without love, how else could it be? You taught me that.'

She was silent, and nervousness brought him to his feet.

'You do still love me, don't you, Caroline? Why won't you admit it?'

'My "old friend" wouldn't like it if I did.'

He knew instantly that she was thinking of their last meeting in Marbella.

'What a fool you must have thought me,' he said savagely. 'But I was so tormented by jealousy, I couldn't think straight.'

'So when did you start straightening your corkscrew mind?' she demanded sarcastically.

'I don't know—I'll be honest about that. But bit by bit I started to see how empty my whole life was. Then I began to think about the sort of person you were and why I loved *you* and no one else. Soon after that I realised you'd never marry a man just for security.'

'I'm delighted by your testimonial, Matt. I may ask you to put it in writing for me one day.'

'I'll do it now,' he said quietly. 'My signature on our wedding certificate. My life in your hands.' He leaned over her and caught them, drawing them to his lips. 'You're everything I dreamed of and never hoped to find.'

Though touched by his words, she was determined not to give in to him. There was a great deal more he still had to confess.

'Caroline, *please*.' He pulled her into his arms and she went, unresisting, accepting that he was too strong for her to fight. 'Say you love me. Say it!'

Her trembling body answered for her, but when he went to kiss her, she turned her head away sharply.

'No, Matt. I do love you—I can't deny it—but I'll never marry you.'

She expected him to argue; to shout and storm around the room, even to make violent love to her. Instead he released her and stepped back, his mouth moving as if he were in pain.

'Very well. If that's the way you feel ... I can understand it, but I won't accept it. I'll start courting you properly, a real old-fashioned wooing—flowers and chocolates and weekends with your uncle and aunt. Everything straight and above board, the way you deserve.'

Caroline was almost too amazed to speak, and forcibly had to restrain herself from rushing into his arms. But he had still not told her the total truth about his behaviour, and until he did, she would remain unbending.

'I can't stop you from trying, Matt.' She went to the door. 'But you won't succeed.'

'I'm a fighter.'

She turned the handle.

'Caroline!' His voice was urgent. 'There's something else I have to say. Something else you should know.'

Her heart started to beat faster and she remained by the door.

'I don't know how to begin,' he muttered, and took an angry pace around the room. 'Until I met you I believed every woman had her price. But you were different. You played hard to get and to my amazement there was nothing I could do to break down your resistance. That made me all the more determined to have you. Marriage never entered my head, as you know, and since I knew you wouldn't accept money to live with me, I had to be devious.' He paused and ran his tongue over his lips, as if it were an effort to talk. 'When Mark told me Tom was in money trouble, I suddenly saw a way of getting you. I told Mark I'd give him the money to settle Tom's debts, providing he could get you to accept my proposal, and I made sure Mark gave Tom the impression it was going to be a proposal of marriage—although I was careful not to include that word on the contract you signed.' Matt gave her an anguished look. 'That's the sort of bastard I am.'

Her eyes glittered with unshed tears. 'Why didn't you tell me all this before when I walked out on you?'

'I was too angry. When you repaid Mark, I thought you'd got the money from another man.'

'I did,' she said. 'An advertising executive.'

'I wish you'd told me.'

'I wanted to hurt you. And you were so quick to believe the worst of me.'

'I'd got into the habit of believing the worst of women,' he said. 'I've been in hell since we parted.' He moved towards her, then stopped. 'You probably despise me even more now than you did before. But I had to tell you the whole truth. I didn't want to begin again with you unless it could be a totally open relationship. I'll let you simmer down a bit before I start knocking at the door again.'

'I've known for a long while that you were behind Mark's offer,' she said bluntly.

'*What?* Who told you?'

Briefly she explained about Tom returning to the yacht for his watch, and overhearing Matt talking to Mark.

'From then on,' she concluded, 'I vowed to make you pay for your behaviour—and I don't mean with money, Matt, but with wounded pride. I played you for a fool. I got drunk deliberately on that first night, and I took sleeping pills to make sure I collapsed.'

'*Deliberately?*' he repeated.

'Yes. And I deliberately added chervil to the coq au vin because I knew you were allergic to it.'

'I suppose you also deliberately fell on the bar of soap and gave yourself a slipped disc?'

'I didn't slip my disc—luckily. But I did step on to the soap with my eyes wide open.'

Matt glared at her in fury, then a gleam appeared in his eyes and his shoulders began to move, slightly at first, but gaining momentum until he was shaking with laughter. Caroline watched him, then she too began to laugh, collapsing on the bed in a paroxysm of near-hysteria.

Only as Matt's arms came round her did her laughter cease. He was beside her on the bed, his thighs heavy on hers as he pressed her down.

'I deserved every single thing you did,' he muttered against her cheek. 'It looks as if I've met my match in you!'

She raised a hand and stroked the side of his face. 'I'm glad you know the truth. The only part I regret was giving you that chervil. I'd no idea you would have such a horrible reaction.'

'So you had a conscience about it, eh? I'm glad to hear it.' His mouth hovered inches above hers. 'Do you forgive me about Mark? That's much more important for me to know.'

'I forgave you the very instant you told me about it. That's all I was waiting for, Matt—for you to tell me the truth.'

'I see.' He gave a deep sigh and relaxed upon her. 'So I can start wooing today?'

'Providing you finish it by the end of the week,' she said demurely. 'I don't think I can hold out longer than that.'

'I'm damn sure I can't,' he said fervently. 'Tell me, my little wretch, what's Plan Four going to be?'

'Surrender,' she said promptly, and deftly twisted from under him to stand by the side of the bed.

He half-turned and lay on his back, watching her from beneath mocking brows. 'Tell me, Caroline, do you love me as much as I love you?'

The question surprised her. 'I can only answer for myself, Matt. I love you with all my heart. I won't say any more. I'll let the years show you.'

'Show me now.' With slow gestures he undid his jacket and loosened his tie. 'Prove it by letting me make love to you.'

Warmth flooded through her body. She wanted to resist him, yet she did not want him to think she did not trust him to marry her. She *did* trust him. Eyes lowered, she slipped off her shoes and crept on to the bed again.

'Yes, Matt,' she whispered, 'I will.'

'Thank you, my darling, but the answer is no.' Smoothly he swung off the bed and caught her up with him, hugging her in a rib-breaking embrace. 'Definitely no,' he repeated. 'I have no intention of letting you take advantage of me like that! Before you get me on a bed again, sweet Caroline, you'll have to make an honest man of me!'

Laughing, she gave him her lips. 'Whenever you say, Matt, whenever you say.'

ROMANCE

Variety is the spice of romance

Each month, Mills & Boon publish new romances. New stories about people falling in love. A world of variety in romance – from the best writers in the romantic world. Choose from these titles in April.

AN ELUSIVE DESIRE Anne Mather
SUP WITH THE DEVIL Sara Craven
ONE WHO KISSES Marjorie Lewty
ONE MORE TIME Karen van der Zee
A MOUNTAIN FOR LUENDA Essie Summers
PHANTOM MARRIAGE Penny Jordan
CAPTIVE LOVING Carole Mortimer
MASTER OF MORLEY Kay Thorpe
SOMEWHERE TO CALL HOME Kerry Allyne
DARK SEDUCTION Flora Kidd
SECOND TIME AROUND Elizabeth Oldfield
THE TYCOON'S LADY Kay Clifford

On sale where you buy paperbacks. If you require further information or have any difficulty obtaining them, write to: Mills & Boon Reader Service, PO Box 236, Thornton Road, Croydon, Surrey CR9 3RU, England.

Mills & Boon
the rose of romance